THE HARSH TRUTH

The human instinct for self-preservation is strong. I know, because mine pulls at me, too, like the needle on a compass. And everybody—I've been reading some philosophy—everybody seems to agree that the instinct and responsibility of all humans is to take care of themselves first. You have the right to survive, if you can.

But how come there don't seem to be any rules about when you ought to help others survive? Rules telling you when that's worth some risk to yourself? Callie and I were working so hard for you, Emmy, but as far as I could see, nobody else cared at all. For any of us.

ALSO BY NANCY WERLIN

Double Helix
Black Mirror
Locked Inside
The Killer's Cousin
Are You Alone on Purpose?

the rules of survival

NANCY WERLIN

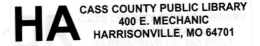
speak
An Imprint of Penguin Group (USA) Inc.

SPEAK
Published by the Penguin Group
Penguin Group (USA) Inc., 345 Hudson Street, New York, New York 10014, U.S.A.
Penguin Group (Canada), 90 Eglinton Avenue East, Suite 700,
Toronto, Ontario, Canada M4P 2Y3 (a division of Pearson Penguin Canada Inc.)
Penguin Books Ltd, 80 Strand, London WC2R 0RL, England
Penguin Ireland, 25 St Stephen's Green, Dublin 2, Ireland
(a division of Penguin Books Ltd)
Penguin Group (Australia), 250 Camberwell Road, Camberwell, Victoria 3124, Australia
(a division of Pearson Australia Group Pty Ltd)
Penguin Books India Pvt Ltd, 11 Community Centre,
Panchsheel Park, New Delhi - 110 017, India
Penguin Group (NZ), 67 Apollo Drive, Rosedale, North Shore 0632, New Zealand
(a division of Pearson New Zealand Ltd)
Penguin Books (South Africa) (Pty) Ltd, 24 Sturdee Avenue,
Rosebank, Johannesburg 2196, South Africa

Registered Offices: Penguin Books Ltd, 80 Strand, London WC2R 0RL, England

First published in the United States of America by Dial Books,
a member of Penguin Group(USA) Inc., 2006
Published by Speak, an imprint of Penguin Group (USA) Inc., 2008

5 7 9 10 8 6

THE LIBRARY OF CONGRESS HAS CATALOGED THE DIAL EDITION AS FOLLOWS:
Werlin, Nancy.
The rules of survival / Nancy Werlin.
p.   cm.
Summary: Seventeen-year-old Matthew recounts his attempts, starting at a young age,
to free himself and his sisters from the grip of their emotionally
and physically abusive mother.
ISBN: 0-8037-3001-2(hc)
[1. Child abuse—Fiction. 2. Brothers and sisters—Fiction. 3. Emotional problems—Fiction.]
I. Title.   PZ7.W4713Ru 2006   [Fic]—dc22   2006001675

Speak ISBN 978-0-14-241071-4

Printed in the United States of America

This book is for all the survivors. Always remember:
The survivor gets to tell the story.

Dear Emmy,

As I write this, you are nine years old, too young to be told the full and true story of our family's past, let alone be exposed to my philosophizing about what it all meant. I don't know how old you'll be when you do read this. Maybe you'll be seventeen, like I am now. Or maybe much older than that—in your twenties or even thirties.

I have decided to write it all down for you, and I will, but that decision doesn't keep me from having doubts. I wonder if maybe it would be better if you never read this. I wonder if you really need to know exactly what happened to us—me, you, Callie—at the hands of our mother. As I sit here writing, part of me hopes that you go along happily your whole life and never need or want to know the details. I believe that's what Aunt Bobbie hopes for, and Callie. I can understand that. For example, I have to admit that I don't want to know any details about what happened when our mother kidnapped you—so long as you've forgotten it, anyway. So long as you're not having screaming nightmares or something.

But if you are reading this letter, that means you

are about to find out everything I know. It means I will have decided to tell you—decided twice. Once, by writing it all down now. And then again, by giving this to you to read sometime in the future.

I hope my memories of that time won't always be as clear as they are now. As I write, I only have to focus and I'm there again, in the past. I'm thirteen and fourteen and fifteen—or younger. It was terrible living through it the first time, but I think it's going to be almost as bad to live through it once more on paper. To try . . . not just to get it all down accurately, but to understand it. I need to make sense of it. I need to try to turn the experience into something valuable for you, and for myself—not just something to be pushed away and forgotten.

Emmy, the events we lived through taught me to be sure of nothing about other people. They taught me to expect danger around every corner. They taught me to understand that there are people in this world who mean you harm. And sometimes, they're people who say they love you.

Matthew

1

MURDOCH

For me, the story begins with Murdoch McIlvane.

I first saw Murdoch when I was thirteen years old. Callie was eleven, and Emmy, you were only five. Back then, you talked hardly at all. We weren't even sure if you'd be able to start school when you were supposed to in the fall. Don't misunderstand—we knew you were smart. But school, well, you know how they are, wanting everybody to act alike.

That particular night in August, it was over a hundred degrees, and so humid that each breath felt like inhaling sweat. It was the fourth day of a heat wave in Boston, and over those days, our apartment on the third floor of the house in Southie had become like the inside of an oven. However, it was a date night for our mother—Saturday— so we'd been locked in.

"I want my kiddies safe," Nikki had said.

Not that the key mattered. Once Callie and I heard you snoring—a soft little sound that was almost like a sigh—we slipped out a window onto the back deck, climbed down the fire escape, and went one block over to the Cumberland Farms store. We wanted a breath of air-conditioning, and we were thinking also about Popsicles. Red ones. I had a couple dollars in my pocket from the last time I'd seen my father. He was always good for a little bit of money, and the fact that it was just about all he was good for didn't make me appreciate the cash less.

It wasn't really his fault, that he was so useless. My dad was afraid of our mother. He kept out of her way. On the few occasions they were in the same room together, he wouldn't even meet her eyes. I didn't blame him for it too much. I understood. She was unpredictable.

I remember that night so well.

"We have to bring a Popsicle back for Emmy," Callie said, her flip-flops slapping against the pavement. "We can put it in the freezer for tomorrow."

I grunted. I didn't think there was enough money for three Popsicles, but if Callie wanted to sacrifice her own for you, knowing you would drip half of it onto your shirt, that was her business. For me, it was hard enough knowing that we couldn't stay long at the store, or even out on the street, where there was sometimes a breeze from the ocean a few blocks away. If you woke up and found you were alone, you might be scared. I'd decided we'd risk being away fifteen minutes. I glanced at my watch; it was only just before eight thirty and the sun hadn't quite gone below the horizon.

Doubt suddenly pushed at me. If you woke—or if our mother returned unexpectedly—

"Don't worry. Emmy won't wake up," Callie said. When it came to you, little sister, we always knew what the other was thinking. "And we'll be right back."

"Okay," I said. But I made a mental note to get us back in ten minutes rather than fifteen. Just in case. And next time, I'd let Callie go to the store alone. She was old enough, really. I'd stay with you. Or bring you, maybe.

It was hard to figure out what would be the safest thing to do, for all three of us, all the time. But it was my job. As we pushed open the door to the Cumberland Farms and were greeted by a glorious blast of cool air, I was thinking that in a year—year and a half—I could maybe go out by myself at night and trust Callie with you. Even if I could only do that once in a while, it would really help. I could get over to the ocean at night, walk the causeway, hang out with some of the guys from school. Maybe I could even talk to this one girl I sort of liked. If our mother were out anyway, it would be okay to leave you girls alone, I thought. I'd still be careful that you weren't alone with her when she came home after her Saturday night outings. That wouldn't be hard, considering she rarely came home before two or three in the morning. If at all.

Then I saw him. Murdoch. Okay, I saw him but I didn't really see him. That came a few minutes later. I just glanced around the store. There was a teenager at the cash register behind the front candy counter. A huge, barrel-shaped man stood in front of the counter with a little boy, smaller even than you were then. And Murdoch (of course I didn't know his name then) and his date (a woman I never saw again) were in line behind the man with the boy.

Callie and I headed straight for the ice cream freezer, and we'd just reached it when the yelling began. We whipped around.

It was the barrel-shaped man and the little kid. The man had grabbed the boy by the upper arms and yanked him into the air. He was screaming in his face while the kid's legs dangled: *"What did you just do?"*

The little kid was clutching a package of Reese's Pieces and he started keening, his voice a long, terrified wail, his small body rigid.

The big man—his father?—shook him hard, and kept doing it.

"I'll teach you to take things without permission! Spend my money without asking!"

And then the other man, the one I later knew was called Murdoch, was between the father and son. Murdoch snatched the little kid away from his father and

4

put the kid down behind him. Then Murdoch swiveled back.

Emmy, I like to freeze the memory in my mind and just look at Murdoch. He was a medium kind of man. Medium height, medium build, hair shaved close to the skull. You wouldn't look twice—until you have looked twice.

He wasn't afraid. I noticed that right away about him. Here was this huge enraged man, facing him. But this other man, Murdoch, was calm. At the same time, there was this tension coiling off him.

Callie and I were behind Murdoch and to the left, so we had only a partial view of his face and expression. But we had a full-on view of the barrel-shaped man. And we had a good view of the little kid, who was so shocked that he stopped crying and just stared up at Murdoch's back with his mouth open.

Meanwhile, Murdoch said, quietly but audibly, "If you want to hurt somebody, you can hurt me. Go on. Hit me. I won't hit back. You can do it until you're not angry anymore. I'll let you."

There was an endless, oh, five seconds. The father's eyes bulged. His fists were clenched. He drew one arm back. But Murdoch was still looking straight at him, and I knew—you could feel it vibrating in the air—that even though Murdoch had said he wouldn't hit him, he wanted to. He wanted to hurt him.

I liked him for that. No, Emmy, I loved him for that. Immediately.

5

"Hit me," Murdoch said. "Come on. Better me than the kid. Why not? You want to."

And then it was all over. The man blinked and took a step back. He said something, loudly, about having had a hard day and it doesn't hurt a kid to learn to keep his hands to himself. And Murdoch was nodding even though I guessed that he was thinking what I was about that man. But Murdoch turned away from the father as if he was no threat anymore. He knelt on the floor in front of the little kid.

You could smell the kid's fear floating on the stale, air-conditioned store air. He stole one little look behind Murdoch at the big man, and you could see him thinking, *I'll have to pay for this later.*

But Murdoch talked directly to the kid. "It's wrong for anybody ever to hurt you. No matter who does it, it's wrong. Can you remember that?"

The kid's eyes were now huge. He looked at his father again. Then back at Murdoch. Then he nodded.

"You'll remember that?" Murdoch insisted. "You don't have to do anything else. You just have to remember."

He waited.

The kid nodded. Solemnly.

"Good," said Murdoch.

The kid reached out one hand toward him. In it was the package of Reese's Pieces. Murdoch took it and said, "Thank you." He stood up in one smooth motion. He put the package on the counter. But his eyes didn't leave the little boy. The little boy kept looking back, too, while the

6

big man finished paying for his stuff and then hustled the kid outside.

As the door slammed behind them, there was complete silence in the store. It was then I realized that Callie had grabbed my hand and was holding it.

"Oh, hello?" said the woman who was with Murdoch. "Hello, Murdoch? You should have thought about me. What if there was a big fight and I got hurt? What kind of a date do you think that would be? Huh? Murdoch? Are you listening to me? Murdoch!"

Murdoch, I thought. It was a name I had never heard before. A strange name.

It suited him.

Murdoch didn't reply. His eyes had narrowed into slits. He held up the pack of Reese's Pieces and said to the teenage clerk, "I'll take these. And the ice coffee." The woman sighed and shrugged. She moved a step closer to Murdoch, but without even looking at her, he took a step away.

One more moment from my memory of that night: On his way out the door, Murdoch turned. He tossed the Reese's Pieces underhand to me and Callie. He smiled at us as he did it, but the smile didn't reach his eyes. And he wasn't thinking about us at all, or really seeing us. I could tell. Not the way he'd seen that little boy.

He was still giving off that invisible coiled pulse of—whatever it was.

He was still angry.

Then he was gone.

2

ABOUT FEAR

I don't know if you'll understand this, Emmy, but for me, fear isn't actually a bad thing. It's a primitive instinct that's your friend. It warns you to pay attention, because you're in danger. It tells you to do something, to act, to save yourself.

I read a book about this recently. If you remind me, I'll give it to you. The guy who wrote it, he's a security expert, the kind of person celebrities and politicians hire to keep them safe from crazies. He says that the ability to become aware of fear is a gift. That if you honor that gift—if you notice when you're afraid and if you respond to your fear instead of ignoring it, you will be safer. Run, he says, run when your fear tells you to.

But he doesn't talk about what happens to your gift of fear when you live with the feeling all the time.

I remember one night, when I was little. I waited until our mother had gone to bed, and then I sneaked into the kitchen. There was a package of Oreo cookies there. My plan was to take one of them back to bed with me. She wouldn't notice one missing cookie, would she? I would eat quietly. And I would make sure not a crumb escaped as evidence.

I made it all the way back to bed with the cookie. I was beneath the sheet, in a little tent, with the cookie flat on my palm and my nose pressed to it—when she whipped back the covers.

"Thief!" our mother yelled. "Cookie thief!" She burst into giggles.

She had the big kitchen knife, and it was pressed to my throat. And as she laughed, I could feel it shake in her hands, and push against my skin.

She cut me that night. Just a little.

Just to teach me not to steal, and not to sneak.

This is what I think happens when you live with fear, and I think it happened to me, to Callie, and to you, even though you were so little. I think the fear gets into your blood. It makes your subatomic particles twist and distort. You change, chemically. The fear changes, too. It becomes not your helper, but your master. You are a slave to it.

Obviously, I am not a scientist. I'm not even sure I would have passed eleventh-grade chemistry if Callie hadn't helped me study. But I know that I am not who I was supposed to be, who I could have been, and I know it's because I was too afraid for too long. It made me think about things I never should have.

I learned to live with the fear. I learned to function with it. We all did. Maybe that was what I recognized in Murdoch that night. Maybe that was what drew me to him. He wasn't afraid. Or—if he was—he took action anyway.

Yes. Where most people would have done nothing, he acted.

Anyway, I stood in that convenience store on that hot summer night and stared after him, and I thought: *I have to know that man.* There is a word for this feeling, Emmy. It's called obsession.

I was obsessed with Murdoch, Emmy, for months before our mother ever dated him. In fact, if not for me, she never would have met him.

3

MY FIRST MEMORY

I must have been about four, and that means Callie would have been two, or a little older, sleeping across the bedroom in her crib. Emmy, you didn't exist yet.

I don't know what time it was. It was the middle of the night, and suddenly I was awake. My every muscle was rigid. I was listening while, at the other end of the apartment, our mother began, without speaking or yelling, to smash one of the kitchen chairs repeatedly against the wall.

And then another one.

Of course, at the time, I didn't know what she was doing, exactly. The next morning, I would go into the kitchen to see the chairs in splintered pieces all over the floor, beneath the gaping hole in the plaster of the wall. In the night, though, I didn't know what was happening,

11

or why, or even exactly where. But I knew who was doing it: Mom. And that was all that mattered.

I don't remember any feeling of surprise. What I remember is the awareness that I had a job to do. Callie had already woken up and started whimpering, and I knew she would start screaming soon. Our mother would hear her—and remember us.

I slipped out of my bed. I worked the mechanism to lower the crib's slatted side, and I clambered up and over it. I grabbed Callie and held her. I whispered, "Shhh, Callie. Shhh."

Holding Callie as she thrashed and yelled into my shoulder, and, eventually, quieted, I felt hope. This wasn't over yet, but I was doing well. I was making sure Callie's yowls couldn't be heard outside our room, over the methodical, determined smashing from the kitchen. If we were lucky—I remember thinking—Callie and I would be left alone, unremembered, and it was my job to try to make that happen.

That particular night, I did it. I kept us out of the way, unnoticed. So, in fact, you could say that my very first memory is one of success. Of triumph. Of watching Callie go back to sleep safely, because I had made sure she hadn't called attention to us while our mother was angry.

I did this many times for you, too, Emmy. So did Callie.

4

SEARCHING FOR MURDOCH

I looked for Murdoch for the rest of my thirteenth year. The first thing I did was go back to the convenience store to ask the teenage clerk if he had seen that man before, or if he knew whether he lived nearby, or if he knew anything at all about him. But the guy didn't have a clue, and he started to look at me funny, so I couldn't ask him to please call me if he saw him again or learned anything about him. In my pocket, I curled my fist around the piece of paper I'd prepared with my name and phone number, crumpling it. But I wasn't discouraged.

I thought Murdoch might be one of the new, young, wealthy people who were moving into our neighborhood, attracted by its nearness to the beachfront, the airport, and the center of Boston. Our mother and her friends complained bitterly about these people, who were cramming the tight city streets of the old neighborhood with their Land Rovers and BMWs. Their presence had driven up housing prices and pushed out most of the old-time working class Irish-American population. We'd have been among those forced to move far out of Boston, according to Aunt Bobbie—who lived alone downstairs in the second-floor apartment. But our grandfather had bought the triple-decker house back when prices were much lower.

"The only good move he made in his entire life," Aunt Bobbie said. "Besides dropping dead before he could gamble the house out from under us."

In those days, every now and then, Aunt Bobbie would talk wistfully about what the house was worth, about how its three apartments could be gutted by a real estate developer and turned into condominiums with walk-in closets and gleaming hardwood floors. But our mother wasn't interested in selling and moving away from the city. Since she and Bobbie had inherited the house jointly, Bobbie had to content herself with raising the rent on the first-floor apartment, where three or maybe even four UMass-Boston college boys were always crammed in, and with her daily monitoring of Southie real estate prices in the newspaper.

I didn't think Murdoch had grown up in Southie. The woman he'd been with had certainly had the local look and sound, but he hadn't. I prayed he hadn't just been visiting her. I hoped he was one of the new people. If he wasn't, I might never find him again.

I went on long walks, scanning every passing face. I visited the convenience store as often as I could. When I could manage it, I showed up there on Saturday nights for at least a few minutes between eight and nine. I took you, Emmy, and we rode the local buses at rush hour so I could stare out the windows at the crowds. I made you and Callie spend long hours with me at Castle Island, next to the port of Boston, because nearly everyone in Southie went there to walk the causeway or fish off the dock or get a tan on the beach or buy an ice cream cone at Sullivan's.

In the early days, I saw Callie watching me as I scanned the face of every man who was about the right height and shape, and eventually she said to me, quietly, "You're looking for him, aren't you?" I nodded. Neither of us had to specify who was meant by "him."

"Why?" Callie asked.

"I don't know," I said. Then: "I just want to know him."

Callie nodded.

But summer ended, and then fall, and then we went through one of the most bitter and miserable winters imaginable—and I don't mean just the weather—and I did not find him.

And so, as spring inched back into Boston and green buds appeared on the neighborhood's few trees, I turned fourteen and, to celebrate my new maturity, I gave up.

5

MY BIRTHDAY PRESENT

It was a May afternoon, and Callie, now twelve to my fourteen, pounded up the stairs and burst into the bedroom I used to share with her and you. You were working with your sticker book on the lower bunk while I did some school reading about the rainforests of Brazil and imagined a struggle between our mother and a python.

"Matt! Look!" Callie was practically hopping up and down. She thrust a piece of paper toward me.

It was a print screen from an online telephone and address directory. Murdoch McIlvane, it said. 892 East Tenth Street, South Boston, Massachusetts. And there was a phone number.

17

The address was only a few streets away, near the beach. How had Callie—

"It's him, Matt," Callie was saying. "I found the address last week, and I've gone over to East Tenth Street every day after school since then, and I hung out and waited. I didn't want you to be disappointed. But today, finally, I saw him."

I was speechless.

"It's a birthday present, Matthew. Just a couple weeks late." Callie's voice was filled with joy and pride.

I found my own voice. "Thanks."

"You're welcome."

It took me a minute before I could take her hand and squeeze it. "How'd you find him? This is incredible."

She hopped from foot to foot. "Well, of course I was looking for him everywhere I went, like you, just hoping to get lucky. But then last week, I realized I could look for him online."

"But without a last name—"

"Not a problem." Callie dropped my hand and spun around three times on the carpet. "Guess why not."

"Callie. Just tell me."

"C'mon, dummy. Guess!"

"Callie."

It turned out Callie had simply gone to an online phone book, typed "Murdoch" in the first name field and "Massachusetts" in the state field, and then methodically gone through the alphabet for the last name, Aa to Mc.

18

"It wasn't like he was named John—or Matthew." She grinned, proud of herself. "There was only one other person named Murdoch in the whole state. Of course, I stopped when I found our Murdoch. I'm really glad his last name didn't begin with a W."

"You're a genius," I said.

She said eagerly, "So, tomorrow's Saturday. What time do you want to go over to East Tenth and meet him?"

My jaw dropped.

"I think we should just go ring his doorbell," Callie said. "If he's home, we could invite him to go for a walk on the causeway with us. Tell him we want to be friends."

So much for genius. Callie didn't understand how to act. "We can't do that."

"Why not?"

"Because . . . because . . ."

I hadn't actually thought past finding Murdoch. I didn't know what my next move should be. Maybe to do what Callie had, just hang around on his street and watch for him. Follow him—learn more. *Then* try to engineer a meeting. The right kind of meeting.

"I want to go slow," I said. When Callie scowled, I waved the piece of paper and added, "Look, is this my birthday present or isn't it?"

"Well, it is, but—"

"Then I get to decide what I do with it, right?"

Callie rolled her eyes. "The address is your present. Not the man. I want to be his friend, too."

19

"Callie."

"Oh, fine. Do it your way. Just don't come running to me for ideas when—"

We heard the apartment door open. Footsteps followed—our mother's. She called our names. Once. Again. Louder.

And then, there she was. In our room, leaning over my shoulder, and reaching out with interest to take the piece of paper with Murdoch's name and address on it from my hand.

"What are you kids up to? And hey, what's this?"

6

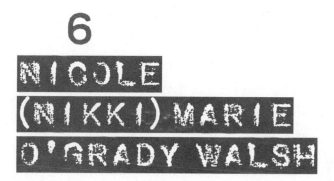

NICOLE (NIKKI) MARIE O'GRADY WALSH

God's honest truth, Emmy: I don't think I was ever able to look at our mother and just see her. Instead, I'd see in my memory the things she did over the years and the expression on her face when she did them. So I could never quite believe that strangers didn't run screaming down the street at the very sight of her.

But they didn't.

What they saw when I was fourteen and she was thirty-five was a pretty woman, I guess. She was of medium height, with pale skin and a good figure—okay, a great figure—that she liked to show off. She changed her hair color all the time, from the palest shades of ash blond to darker blond mixes, and sometimes all the way over into red. Once it was even a Halloween orange.

My father, Ben, says that when they were young and in high school together, Nikki's hair was a wonder, hanging to her waist in long, lustrous, rich-brown strands. He says it floated around her when she walked. I remember this hair, because when Callie went to kindergarten and came home saying she had learned there were twelve inches in a foot, Nikki grabbed a tape measure and stretched out on the living room carpet, her hair flowing above her. She made Callie measure it, roots to ends. It was less than a full yard long, I remember. This made Nikki very, very angry. She ended up cutting Callie's hair almost to the scalp to show her how important hair was to a woman. Callie hid her head under baseball caps the rest of that summer, so that the bald patches wouldn't show.

Ironically, shortly after that, Nikki cut her own hair to shoulder-length. I guess that made it easier to dye.

She preferred to wear tight jeans, or her favorite, black leather pants. She always chose tops in vivid colors like green and purple, in slinky or clingy fabrics. With her jeans, she always wore the same belt, which had a chunky, heavy brass buckle ornament in the shape of a Celtic cross. She liked wearing high heels, too, and boots.

Nikki wore lipstick and eyeliner every day. You had to work hard to see her eyes. She always had a sweep of hair in the way, and then she'd lift her hand and pretend to brush it back.

Do you remember at all, Emmy? Her eyelids folded up into their sockets so neatly that it looked like she didn't have any.

7
PORTUGUESE
SEAFOOD PAELLA

Our mother took the piece of paper from me. There was no point trying to keep it from her. Just before she came into the room, it had flashed into my mind to shove the address into my pocket, to protect it until I knew what I wanted to do with it. But I hadn't. I wasn't sure why not. She read aloud, breezily, "Murdoch McIlvane, 892 East Tenth Street. So, who's this guy?"

"Nobody," Callie said. "It's just—he's just this guy." She stopped, at a loss. She looked at me.

"You wouldn't like him," I said to our mother.

She didn't pursue it, not yet, anyway. She shrugged and leaned over toward you, Emmy, pulling you backward up off the bunk and into her arms. "Emmy! Is there

24

a big hug for Mommy from her baby? A big kiss for Mommy?"

The piece of paper was now bunched up in her hand against your butt. Meanwhile, your dangling left arm was being squeezed between our mother's body and the edge of the upper bunk—maybe deliberately, maybe not; it was hard to tell. You looked at Callie and me from over our mother's shoulder. You had a sticker on your cheek, a little bee. Your lower lip was trembling. I hoped you wouldn't try to wriggle out of the embrace, because in fact our mother seemed to be in quite a good mood. She was humming.

Cocaine? New man? There were a few possibilities, and I didn't care which one it was. Maybe we'd have an okay evening. As for Murdoch's address . . . well, we'd see.

Nikki was dancing you around the room, so at least your arm was free, though I could see a red crease mark running across it just above the elbow. "We're celebrating tonight," our mother said. "Rachel at work quit. I was thinking about making Portuguese seafood paella. I brought home everything we need. Unless paella would be too sophisticated for you kids? I hope you're going to appreciate all the work that has to go into it."

"It'll be fine," I said, while at the exact same moment, Callie said, "Whatever you want."

Murmuring "Yum yum yum!" our mother waltzed you—and Murdoch's address—out of the bedroom.

Callie gripped my arm. "I'll print you out another one," she whispered.

"I already memorized it," I whispered back.

"She won't—" Callie stopped. "I don't know, go meet him?"

"She'll do whatever she does," I said. "Let's go after them."

But Callie still had my arm. "I'm sorry. I wasn't thinking. I could have memorized the address and just told you."

"And I could have hidden it. I guess I wasn't fast enough." I shrugged. I tried to pull my arm away, but Callie said, "Wait a second. Uh—what's paella?"

"Callie," I said, "I'll know when you know."

We hadn't been even a minute talking, but by the time we got to the kitchen, chaos was well under way. Emmy, you had been dumped on the floor, and our mother was tearing into two paper grocery store bags, tossing their contents onto the counter and table, and balling up the remains of the bags and throwing them in the general direction of the garbage can. I stared at what she was putting out on the counter. Along with a package of frozen peas and some cans of soup stock, there were big clear plastic bags of shrimp, mussels, and clams. And some other grayish seafood-type thing I didn't recognize. Ugh.

Okay, Callie and I would choke down whatever, but Emmy, that was when you ate hot dogs, plain macaroni,

Cheerios, baby carrots, cheese toast, grape Popsicles, and (if I bribed you) fish sticks.

Callie had gone to scoop you up, Emmy, so I leaned down to pick up the grocery bags from the floor. Whole Foods, the store near the medical office building where our mother worked. I got a look at the checkout slip. It was $128.63, for two bags of groceries that contained nothing a picky little girl would eat.

"Matthew?" Our mother was scowling at me, her hands on her hips. "What exactly are you doing?"

I knew my face was still perfectly bland. I nodded at the crumpled paper bags and receipt in my hands. "Just throwing these out."

A moment of silence. Then: "I'm warning you. I want to celebrate tonight. I could have gone out with my friends, but I thought it would be good to do something nice for my kids."

A familiar airless feeling had entered the room, the way it always did, suddenly and out of nowhere. From the corner of my eye, I saw Callie retreat a few steps with you in her arms, positioning herself near the doorway so she could get the two of you out of the way if necessary.

"Do you understand?" our mother said.

"Yes," I said. "I'm sorry."

A moment passed. Would she nod and turn away?

No.

"I don't think you do understand, Matthew. I've gone to a lot of trouble already. I bought fresh, good, and interesting food—and no, it wasn't cheap, I saw you looking at the receipt—and I did it for you. It's going to take me a long time to prepare this meal, because it's a special meal and special things take time and care. Most people wouldn't bother. Most people microwave fish sticks or serve cereal for dinner to their kids and think that's good enough. But when I cook for my kids, I make it count. I spend money and take time. And you had better appreciate it."

I knew better than to say what I did say next, but she had stolen my birthday present, Murdoch's phone number.

"What exactly are you trying to tell me, Mom? That you don't want me to throw out the grocery bags?"

She snatched the plastic bag of mussels off the counter and slammed me across the face with it. Once. Twice.

My head had jerked to the right. My cheek stung. I didn't move to touch it, though. I looked into her eyes.

At this point, there was never any way to know what to do. Sometimes she wanted you to confront her. "Act like you have balls, for God's sake." But other times, any show of strength made her angrier and it was better to grovel.

I chose. I shifted my gaze down to the floor and waited, like a good beta monkey.

I saw her feet move. She took one step away. I thought it was over. But then she whirled back and slammed me across the face with the mussels again, on the other cheek. "That's to teach you not to criticize how I keep my kitchen. *My home.*"

And suddenly I had an idea. I dropped the torn and balled-up grocery bags onto the floor.

It worked. When I looked up, she had turned back to her paella.

Air returned to the room.

Over her shoulder, Nikki said conversationally, "So, who's this Murdoch McIlvane guy? You trying to set me up on a date? I was just thinking it was time to find someone new. I'll pay him a visit tomorrow, check him out. I'll tell him my kids set us up." She smiled right at me. "Don't worry. I'll be at my most charming. He'll love me."

I couldn't say anything. I saw Callie looking at me, horrified. I could read her mind. Our mother was going to turn right around and meet Murdoch the way Callie had wanted *us* to do. Wouldn't this ruin everything for us? Ruin the possibility of Murdoch becoming *our* friend? Callie wanted me to stop our mother. Somehow.

But I didn't know how.

I looked away from Callie.

8
MIRACLE SUMMER

When you're living your life in endurance mode, you don't expect anything good to happen. I'm not saying you don't dream about some miracle that would change everything for the better. But you pretty much know it's only a fantasy, and that you have no real control over anything.

So it's a huge shock if a miracle does occur in your life.

I know you remember some of that miracle summer with Murdoch, Emmy, because we've talked about it.

Who would have thought that one of Nikki's embarrassing schemes would have gone so well for her and for us? But it did. The next morning after she took Murdoch's address away from me, Nikki put on a short summer dress and left with you. I only asked Murdoch recently exactly what occurred.

He says Nikki looked him up and down when he opened the door. She had you in her arms, and, smiling over your head, she introduced herself. "Murdoch McIlvane? Listen, I know this'll sound crazy, but someone I know thought I ought to meet you. And so, well, would you like to go over to the L Street diner with me and Emmy for coffee? Right now?"

"I was charmed," Murdoch admitted. "Women usually aren't so direct, and I liked it. She was so pretty, and Emmy was smiling at me. It was just coffee at the diner. I wasn't doing anything. I wasn't seeing anybody. I thought, why not?"

Do you remember that first date between them, Emmy? I suppose that's too much to expect, that you would remember the start of the miracle.

Anyway. Here's something *I* remember.

One Saturday night, during the miracle time—which lasted a little less than three months—Murdoch and Callie and our mother and you and I watched a movie about a prisoner of war. Well, okay, you weren't watching. You were sprawled on top of Murdoch on the sofa, asleep. He had one hand stroking your hair and the other was holding our mother's hand. Callie and I were on the floor with the popcorn and the remote control.

We loved being on the floor. Murdoch had this red and blue rug with a pad underneath it, and big soft cotton pillows to lean on. As I watched the movie, though, I was on the verge of deciding that Murdoch's TV was too small. I was that relaxed.

Anyway, in the war movie, the prisoner guy was locked up in the jungle in a tiny bamboo hut on stilts. The hut was too small for him to stand up or lie down, so all he could do was crouch or sit hunched over in one or two positions. They shoved food in at him every so often, and he, you know, did his business out of a little hole in the floor, and the sun beat down overhead during the day and turned his cage into a stinking oven. The days and weeks and months and years passed, and that was his life. Nobody ever even talked to him.

"Are you kids sorry you picked this movie?" Murdoch asked, after about twenty minutes. He had put it on Pause. "I've got some other movies we could watch instead."

"No," Callie and I chorused together. "It's interesting," I added. I wondered if Callie, like me, was remembering the times we'd been locked in our room . . . especially in the summer.

Murdoch turned to our mother. "What about you, Nikki? Are you okay with this movie for the kids?"

"Sure," said our mother. "Whatever they want."

Murdoch was still frowning. "You kids should know, this isn't made up for Hollywood. This sort of thing really happens to people. The purpose of this particular kind of torture is to make someone lose his mind. It usually works, too." He paused. "It would for me. I'm sure of it. It probably wouldn't even take a month."

We all said we would go crazy, too. We maintained a respectful silence for a minute or two, and then Murdoch, with obvious reluctance, pressed the Play button again.

I don't know about Callie, but I was just agreeing with Murdoch because, even though I was fourteen, I was sort of being a baby. I wanted to dress like Murdoch, act like Murdoch, be like Murdoch. Where he was, I was. What he said, I agreed with. I even would try to get him to talk about what he had been like when he was my age, where he had lived, what his parents had been like. He never had much to say about his childhood or parents and always answered shortly and then changed the subject. I thought if he would only tell me, I could try to be more like him.

But, as I watched this war movie, I wasn't convinced that I would actually go crazy, if it were me in a little jungle hut. Funny how I remember this. I'm not saying that I didn't know that guy had it way worse than Callie and you and me. But I couldn't help thinking that he had some stuff going for him. Predictability. Every day was the same. He didn't go to sleep thinking he might wake up with somebody holding a knife to his throat and giggling. And there wasn't anybody else he had to stick around to protect, either, which meant he had the option of trying to kill his tormentors—or even himself. Certainly he could afford to pursue the survival strategy he chose, which was zoning out. Turn-

ing his mind off until it was needed. Until his miracle ?
happened.

He was luckier than us there, too. His miracle lasted.
By the end of the movie, he was free. Whereas, I always
knew that our miracle wouldn't last. Couldn't. But while
it did . . .

I broke my own rules of survival while it did. I did
things that I knew were stupid and useless, like hoping,
and praying. I got spoiled and cocky and took things for
granted, like that soft carpet and that TV and that nice,
clean, safe apartment with Murdoch cooking stir-fry
chicken for dinner, and always enough milk and juice in
the refrigerator for you, which you appreciated, I knew,
even though you still weren't talking.

I even began to take for granted the way our mother
was during that time. Soft. Laughing. Warm. Reasonable.

You know what I was hoping for? I bet you can guess,
Emmy. I wasn't just hoping for Murdoch to stay with
us. I was hoping I'd wronged Nikki all these years.
That maybe—like us—all she'd ever really needed was
Murdoch. And then she, and we, could all be normal.

It seemed like it could happen, that summer. Miracles
were all around. During week three, when we were all
having dinner at Murdoch's apartment, you held out the
Minnie Mouse mug that Murdoch had bought specially
for you. You waved it imperiously in the air.

"A little more milk, Em?" he asked you.

34

"No, thank you, Murdoch," you said, as if you'd been talking in full, clear sentences all along, as if we'd never worried about whether you'd be able to start school on schedule in the fall. "I just like this mug."

9

ON THE ROCKS

She pretended to be normal, our mother, during most of those weeks she was with Murdoch. She tried hard, which was something I'd never seen in her before and was the thing that made me hope for the impossible. But she didn't, or couldn't, cover up her personality perfectly. There were cracks in her behavior, times when her true self would seep through the veneer of warmth and merriment like water into a basement. I watched Murdoch to see if he would notice. To see if he would understand what he saw. To see what he would do then.

A weak man would be hypnotized, paralyzed. (As far as I can tell, this was what happened to my father, Ben, when he met Nikki as a teenager.) A bad man would be attracted to her on a more equal basis. And a good man, of course, would run like hell.

Murdoch eventually ran. But not at first. At first, it seemed to me that he was just puzzled. Like I said, Nikki was trying. And frankly, we kids were trying hard, too. We covered up for her, and we also did our best to surround Murdoch with appreciation and, well, love. We wanted him to want to be with us. We wanted him to want us.

I sort of cringe to remember it. We were pretty pathetic. But he did like us. It was obvious he did—obvious that he liked kids. His invitations to Nikki almost always included all three of us. Only rarely did they go out alone together at night, to a club or a party or a nice restaurant, the kind of things she liked to do. He wanted to take us all to the ball game, or the aquarium, or to have a barbecue in his backyard. She'd be dressing to go out for a drink at eleven at night, and he'd be yawning.

Nikki played along with this for a while, but I think she got really tired of it. Then came her first major slipup.

It was a Sunday afternoon in late July, and Murdoch had taken us all on a picnic to Gloucester. We set up by the ocean on huge flat rocks. Below us, a steep incline ran down to the water. We ate and talked idly and watched the white-capped waves at the base of the rocks and the soaring, cawing gulls in the blue sky above. We felt the sun and the breeze on our shoulders and faces. We inhaled to smell the difference between the Gloucester air, thirty miles north of the city, and the air at home in Southie.

Just before our mother cracked, I was eating a perfectly ripe peach, leaning over carefully so that the juice dripped down onto the rocks and not my T-shirt. Callie had taken you to examine a little tide pool a few yards across from us on the rocks, and our mother was lying on her side, leaning on one arm, listening to Murdoch and me talk. She had taken off her high-heeled sandals and was wiggling her bare toes with their blue sparkly toenails.

Okay, maybe I did monopolize him and maybe it was dull for her and maybe I should have known better. Maybe I actually did know she was bored and edgy. But I kept Murdoch focused on me anyway as I asked questions about his current job. I didn't ask just because I liked hearing Murdoch talk—although I did—but because I knew he would enjoy talking about it.

Murdoch loved his work as a home building and improvement contractor. He knew all about the details of building; floors and fittings, windows and ceilings, decorative tile and wainscoting, built-in cabinets and perfectly plastered walls. He could get almost poetic about well-planned plumbing and electrical lines. And when he talked about these things, you could feel his competence along with his love for doing them. He liked houses that were all messed up. He liked to fix them, to make them beautiful.

"We salvaged the old wood floors from this house that was being demolished," Murdoch was saying. "It's amazing stuff. Listen, you know what, Matt, I can bring you to the site and show you—"

Nikki suddenly jumped up. "Oh, please! My head's exploding from boredom. Come on, let's have some fun!"

She laughed, and I saw Murdoch smile as he looked up at her, but I knew that laugh of hers. I got up. I wanted to warn Murdoch to get up, too, and to hurry. But it was too late, she'd already run across to the rock pool, grabbed you, Emmy, up under one arm like a football, and raced down the incline, toward the ocean.

Our mother's hair flew out behind her like a flag. She ran from one giant rock to another. She shouted for us to come join her, to show some spirit, to have some fun. Were we alive or were we dead?

Emmy, you screamed. I guess it was a delayed reaction to being seized. Simultaneously, Murdoch was up and yelling, "Nikki! Stop! These rocks aren't safe for running around. This isn't a beach—"

Nikki did stop. She turned and called back to Murdoch: "It's not safe?" She sounded almost reasonable.

"No." Murdoch's brow smoothed out when she turned. "Some of the rocks are unstable down there. It's just not a good place to run around." He'd gotten up, but that was all. I knew he thought she'd stop and just come back. She wasn't very far away yet.

Meanwhile, though, Callie and I had already started down toward you. Murdoch was right—the rocks were unstable; one of them shifted dangerously beneath my feet and I saw Callie slip on another. "Hey!" Murdoch called after us. "Matt, Callie! Didn't you hear me? That's not safe. Come back up here." He began following us, moving quickly, competently.

Below, our mother laughed again. She put you down on your feet, Emmy, and then grabbed your hand and made you run with her, pulling you along by one arm. "Chase us!" she yelled. "Come on! Come on!"

She went from rock to rock, running parallel to the ocean, dragging you. Once you fell and got yanked to your feet, forced to run on.

"Come on! Losers—catch us!"

Do you remember any of this, Emmy?

Callie and I were running, too. It was what Nikki wanted. We had to pretend we were all playing her game; we had to get you back safe—I don't really know why we ran after you, I just know we did. I was terrified; the rocks were slippery and some of them moved when you landed on them, and I was wearing old sneakers without good gripping soles. Callie was barefoot, like Nikki, which was maybe better for gripping, but the rocks were jagged. I could hear her panting beside me. I spared a moment to wonder what Murdoch was thinking, and where he was—

He came even with us and we felt his hands come down on our shoulders, stopping us in our tracks. "*Sit down*. Stay right here!"

He was enraged.

"You don't understand," Callie panted. "Emmy!"

His voice was clipped. "I'll get Emmy. *Stay here.*"

He didn't even dream we'd disobey. He was already past us, running full tilt across the rocks, gaining on our mother and you. "Nikki! Nikki, what do you think you're doing?"

Callie and I exchanged one look and then we started running again. We didn't know what was going to happen, but we knew our mother would do something. She was looking over her shoulder now as she ran. She watched Murdoch as he got closer and closer—

She changed direction, heading farther down the incline toward the ocean where waves smashed against the rocks. At first, Emmy, she dragged you behind her, but as Murdoch gained on you both, she grabbed you up again in her arms. And then, suddenly, you were on the very last rock, next to the edge. A big rock, with what looked to me like a long drop to the churning water below.

Our mother turned so her back was to the water. Murdoch was now only the width of a few large flat rocks away from her. He slowed down and reached out.

"Nikki, look. This isn't a playground. I don't think you understand—"

Two things happened. Beside me, Callie slipped and fell. She yelled, and in a glance I saw that her left foot was cut and bleeding. I reached down to help her up.

And our mother giggled. I looked up to see that she now had you suspended upside down over the churning water at the edge of the rocks.

She was holding you by your ankles.

Murdoch was an arm's reach and a half away. Too far.

And Callie and I, we were too far away, too.

Gently, our mother began to swing you. Out over the water. Back over the rock. Water. Rock.

Water. Rock.

You weren't screaming anymore. If you were making any sound at all, I couldn't hear it. What I *could* hear was the drumming of my blood in my ears as my heart pumped.

Over our heads, the gulls cawed. And then even they were silent.

"Emmy loves this!" Nikki called. "I know what my kids like."

"Nikki." Murdoch's voice carried up to Callie and me. I thought of that moment in the Cumberland Farms store, when Murdoch had faced that angry man.

I held my breath.

I don't know how long we all stood there. Maybe just a minute. Maybe two. Murdoch's eyes were locked on our mother's.

Then: "Just joking," our mother said, and pulled you back up into her arms. "Just having fun. I mean, you're all so serious, so boring. We should have gone to that carnival in Lynn. That would have been more fun than this."

Murdoch didn't answer. He stepped closer, reaching out to take you. Our mother let Murdoch take you from her. She smiled at him.

You were safe in Murdoch's arms. We watched your hands grip at him.

And we watched as our mother again took flight, feinting to the left and darting around Murdoch, running again across the rocks, but this time up, toward the top of the cliff, toward the car.

"You don't know how to have any fun! Any of you!" she called back at us. "Losers!"

Murdoch didn't break up with Nikki right after that. I guess he stayed confused about her several weeks longer. But that was when I knew he would. That the miracle had ended.

10

CALLIE'S DREAM

Maybe a week after that day in Gloucester, I found a piece of paper on which Callie had written out our names:

Murdoch McIlvane
Nicole O'Grady Walsh McIlvane
Matthew Eamon Walsh McIlvane
Callie Suzanne Walsh McIlvane
Emma Mary Walsh McIlvane

I stared at the paper, and I had to force back the acid pushing at my throat. My hands shook.

She had not just written out our names, though. Beneath that, she had written her own, again and again, in variations.

Callie S.W. McIlvane
Callie S. McIlvane
Callie Suzanne McIlvane
Callie McIlvane
C.S. McIlvane
C. McIlvane
Miss McIlvane
Ms. McIlvane
Ms. Callie McIlvane

And finally, after a space, and in letters that were shaky with their own courage:

Dr. Callie McIlvane

It took my breath away, that final name. I had had no idea. I sat there for a while, remembering how Callie had helped me with science homework that year. My homework should have been over her head. And then, too, there was the logical, deductive way she'd located Murdoch.

Dr. Callie McIlvane.

That was when I understood that Callie dreamed bigger than I ever dared. I only wanted us to survive.

45

11

THE BREAKUP

Murdoch broke up with Nikki right after Labor Day weekend in September. He talked to me about it a week later, basically because I went to him and forced him to.

"Matt, try to understand. It wasn't going to work out with her and me. She, well . . . she—" He stopped talking, groping for words that he thought wouldn't be hurtful to me. "Things she liked to do weren't . . . weren't really for me.

"But I liked hanging out with you and your sisters. I like you guys. You know that. I was trying to figure out how to—how to not hurt you, too. Or at least as little as possible."

I had shown up on his doorstep and demanded that he talk to me. My plan was to go all pathetic. Ask him why things couldn't go back to the way they'd been. I was probably a little insane.

But in the end I couldn't say those things to him. I knew we couldn't turn back the clock. He knew I knew. Nobody couldn't know, after what Nikki had done on Labor Day weekend.

The previous big holiday weekend, over the Fourth of July, we had been almost like a family, the five of us. As Labor Day approached, though, we had not seen Murdoch for many days, and our mother had been twitching with suppressed—something. Rage? Lust? Restlessness? On two nights during that week, she'd left us in the apartment alone and gone off, to see Murdoch, she said. She was gone all night. Later, Murdoch said she wasn't with him those nights. But we thought she was. I thought, however sure they were to break up in the end, that it hadn't happened yet. That we would have a little more time with Murdoch.

But Nikki had already fully reverted to someone we hadn't seen since before Murdoch came into our lives. Her eyes were entirely dark, animal. She came home in the morning after one of those nights out, wrecked, dazed, tottering, red-eyed, limping slightly, and with a smile on her mouth. She threw herself into bed to sleep off the night while we crept around so as not to wake her.

I heard her leave two phone messages for Murdoch. She said the kind of things I'd heard her say many times, when she'd been with men who weren't Murdoch. She called in those messages in front of us. She smiled at us while she said those things into the phone.

I could have tried to think it all out then, but I didn't.

47

I didn't want to. I tiptoed around that week and hoped it would pass, hoped Murdoch would come over . . . and fixated on having a barbecue at his place like the one we'd had on the Fourth of July. I took you to the grocery store and we looked at hot dog buns and marshmallows and hamburger patties and talked about how delicious it had all been. There wasn't any corn on the cob in the store. You insisted on looking in every aisle, even though I told you that if it wasn't with the vegetables, it wasn't there at all. Murdoch would get us sweet corn from that farm, I said. Like before, I said.

Murdoch had better not disappoint Emmy, I thought. *It's mean. It's cruel. She expects us to have a barbecue! I told her we would do that. I told her we would have plans!* The tension and fear gathered and gathered inside me, and finally, at home, Friday afternoon, I called Murdoch myself on the prepaid cell phone he had given Callie and me to share because we ought to have it in case of emergency. But he didn't pick up and I found I couldn't leave a message.

He would call. I knew he would call. He would call. Call, call. *Call.*

Call!

And that night, after nine o'clock, our mother came out of her room holding the phone in her hand. She was smiling, flushed, and she was all dressed up to go out— green sequined halter top, tight skirt, high heels. "Come on. We're all going over to Murdoch's."

Callie and I exchanged glad glances. We couldn't possibly have moved faster, even though we had to get you out of bed and dressed. We figured you could go back to sleep at Murdoch's, you'd done it before. Everything was okay again—well, okay enough.

The light was on at Murdoch's house, and his car was in front, so I didn't realize that we weren't expected until he came to the door. I saw his expression as he looked away from our mother and at Callie and you and me. There was surprise on his face, yes, but also something else.

Now, I rarely thought about our aunt Bobbie in those days. She was just the woman who lived downstairs. We said hello and good-bye and little more, since she and Nikki didn't get along. But as I looked at Murdoch in the doorway of his home, I had a feeling of recognition. I'd seen that expression before—on Aunt Bobbie's face, when she looked at us sometimes. I had not known what it was until I saw it on Murdoch's face, too.

It was guilt.

The recognition hit me like a fist in the throat.

He didn't say anything.

Our mother had snatched you up into her arms on the walk over, because you weren't walking fast enough. Now she pushed you at Murdoch and his arms opened automatically to take you. For a second I hated him, even though I also saw, just by how he was holding you, Emmy, that he did care. Despite his intention to leave us.

He looked at me and Callie, too. Just a blink. There was no expression on his face now, at all.

Nikki said, smoothly: "Look, Murdoch, I need help. I've had an emergency call from Rebekah. You haven't met my friend Rebekah. Anyway, she's been in a car accident and I have to go be with her at the hospital. You watch the kids. I don't want to leave them home alone since I'm not sure when I'll be back."

He didn't say anything. Later I asked him if he'd believed her, even for a second, and he'd shrugged. "I don't know." Then, seconds later, and so softly I had to strain to hear: "No."

But that was later. Then, I didn't know what Murdoch thought, only what I knew. And I didn't need to look at Callie to know what she was thinking. There had been no telephone call from Rebekah—the phone hadn't rung at our apartment all night. And as to our mother not wanting to leave us home alone, well, it had never bothered her before.

We said nothing. It was dangerous to contradict her.

Nikki was already turning away. She was practically running. We looked after her. She didn't look back.

We watched Murdoch watch her go. One long second passed. Two. Three.

Then: "You guys had better come in," he said, and we did. But it wasn't the same in his place, as we stayed there Friday night, and Saturday night, and Sunday night, and Monday night, too, with no word from our mother. This time, we had not been invited. This time, we were not wanted. And the days passed, and our mother did not come back, and did not call, and did not come back, and did not call. And Murdoch was kind to us. Even loving. But distant and detached and wary, and—and gone from us.

On Sunday morning, after Murdoch had told us he was going to call the police—he'd already called all the area hospitals and they'd all denied that our mother's friend Rebekah was there—I told him she'd done this before. Disappeared for days. I told him that she'd just be angry if anybody made a fuss. I told him she'd be back when she was ready, and not before.

"I'm sorry," I said. "I wish she'd just left us at home. Not bothered you. We could go back there now. We'll be fine. Aunt Bobbie's away this weekend, but we've stayed alone before when she wasn't right downstairs. Aunt Bobbie doesn't really matter even when she's there."

"No," said Murdoch, after a long moment. "You should stay here. It's okay."

I knew it wasn't okay. But I couldn't say anything else. I couldn't even look him in the eye. I slunk away.

Ironically, we did all the things that weekend, the four of us, that I had hoped we would. Barbecued in his back-yard, while waving across the fence to his neighbor, a woman called Julie. Squeezed into Murdoch's truck and went to the beach in Duxbury. Watched movies together at night, ones Murdoch picked. *Shrek. Mulan.* A very old one called *Swiss Family Robinson,* which you, Emmy, wanted to watch twice.

Murdoch was like a robot. It was unspeakably horrible.

On Wednesday evening, Nikki came back for us. And I watched Murdoch look at her as she trotted into his kitchen wearing the exact same clothes she'd had on five days before. Her arms were covered with bruises, and the first thing she did was come up to Murdoch and throw her arms around him and kiss him, like he was her property.

And now, this will surprise you. It surprised me what I felt as I looked at Murdoch, who stood like a statue in her embrace, before he reached down and simply forced her away from himself, pried her off as if she were a piece of garbage, and stepped decisively away.

It felt as if he was treating us—you, me, and Callie— like garbage, too.

12

FUN, FUN, FUN

In the weeks after Murdoch broke up with our mother, Callie and you and I were involved in a frantic round of enforced family fun. You might remember a little of it, Emmy.

Before, there had been times when Nikki kept us going-going-going from early morning until late at night. But never had it lasted so long or been so intense. I thanked God that at least summer was over and we had the relief of school on the weekdays. Even you were in school—first grade, Emmy. Anyway, I was thinking that surely our mother's merry-go-round would wind down soon. It always had before, when she got tired of us, when she got distracted by something new in life.

This time, though, it seemed to take forever. One crazy Sunday, I remember, we started out at seven a.m. at the pancake house. Waving away the menus, our mother announced to the waitress, "We'll just take a big stack of every kind of pancake you make. We want buttermilk, chocolate chip, banana, blueberry, and pecan—oh, and also a plate of those little silver dollar pancakes, too, just for fun. And then we'd like separate dishes of strawberries and whipped cream—actually, a can of whipped cream if you have it that way—and butter. Oh, and do you have chocolate sauce as well as maple syrup?" She turned to us. "You guys, listen. What we're going to do is put all this stuff in the middle of the table. We'll get plates for all of us, and then we'll make sort of pancake sundaes. Isn't that a great idea? I thought of it last night. Fun, huh?"

"Yes," Callie said, instantly. "Great idea. Wow."

I nodded. "Lots of fun."

There was a little silence. Our mother was now looking at you.

My stomach clenched. "Fun, Emmy," I prompted. "Fun!"

There was a long silence.

Then: "Fun," you said, and you were smiling for real. Despite my own tension, I realized with a shock that it was possible that this *would* be fun for you. After all, once upon a time, this sort of thing had been fun for me.

Callie and I exchanged a glance. Ever so slightly, she shrugged.

"I'm brilliant," said our mother. And then, to the waitress, in a rapid stream of words, she continued: "We'll need more maple syrup, because this little pitcher is only half full. Big glasses of milk for all my kids because I want them to grow up strong. Calcium is very important for growing bones. Oh, so is vitamin C, so we need orange juice, big glasses of that. Coffee for me, though, because I'm bad." She giggled. "That's all. Thanks!"

The waitress left. Nikki lifted her arms and twisted her hair up behind her head, smiling brightly at us. "Isn't this the best idea? And this is only the beginning. Wait until you find out what else I have planned for today. You won't believe how much fun we're going to have."

At the end of the next hour, we had made probably the biggest mess the pancake house had ever seen. I had eaten so much, and it had been so awful after the first two pancakes, that I felt as if I might spew. I blamed Callie. She had eaten a single pancake with only a modest amount of syrup, and simply refused to eat more, causing me to worry that we were going to have a big nasty scene. But instead, Nikki had shrugged and said lightly, "Oh well, I suppose you're dieting. It's not like I never do that." And the tension had passed. But I had felt obligated to eat double to make up for Callie, and to show that I was having a good time, and that this was a great idea. Meanwhile, you, Emmy, got sticky syrup and pancake bits all over yourself, the table, and the floor, and had a simply glorious time. And that made it all better, except—

Except that the day was far from over, and next on Nikki's agenda was picking up a rental car so that we could spend the day at Six Flags amusement park, which was a two-and-a-half-hour drive away. Fifteen minutes down the highway in our rented canvas-topped Jeep, I actually did spew—luckily, Nikki pulled the Jeep over in time—and that set the tone for the rest of my day.

Tilt-A-Whirl. Bumper cars. Three separate roller coasters. Octopus. The Giant Drop. Nikki wanted to go on them all, but most of the time I was able to sit it out with you, because you were too small to go on any of the adult rides. Callie was a trouper and went with Nikki.

"You owe me," she whispered.

"No, *you* owe *me*, for every single pancake I ate this morning."

Also, I was forced to "taste, you have to at least take a taste, aren't you having fun?" cotton candy, a giant hot dog, and nachos.

And then it was necessary for all four of us to go together, as a family, on the rides that you were big enough for. Teacups. The little Ferris wheel. These little boats that went round and round on a rail. Some old-fashioned toy cars that went around a track. And, finally, the carousel, where I climbed onto a silvery blue seahorse that went up and down, up and down, while we went round and round, round and round, until I upchucked the cotton candy, hot dog, and nachos on the seahorse's head. You laughed at me, Emmy.

The worst part of the day was still ahead, though, and it came toward the end of the drive home. It was nearly ten o'clock at night by then, and you were asleep in the backseat of the Jeep with your seat belt undone and your head on Callie's lap. Traffic on the highway was light but steady, and thanks to my touchy stomach, I was up front with Nikki. And so I was the one to whom she said, conversationally, as we drove down the highway, "Tell me how much fun you had today, Matt."

"It was fun."

Even I could hear how dull my voice sounded. I hoped she would let it go. It was late, and she had to be tired, too—she'd driven for hours today in the rented Jeep.

"That sounds convincing."

"It was fun, Mom."

Her voice got harsher. "I know you were sick, but that's just the price you pay for eating like a pig."

"Yeah, that's right. It was my fault."

Callie, from the backseat, said, "We did have fun, Mom." She too sounded more exhausted than happy.

"Really?" Nikki said. "Isn't it strange, then, that I haven't heard a single thank you?"

"Oh—thank you—sorry—thank you—" we both sputtered.

"It's a little late now." Nikki was looking straight ahead as she drove. The road we were on was a major road, almost a highway, but was not divided by any kind of barrier.

Suddenly, Nikki jerked the wheel of the Jeep and took us into the next lane of traffic, the fast one.

"I go to a lot of trouble for you kids," she said. "I love

57

you to death, but this is one of those times when I think I'm not appreciated. Or maybe it's that you think somebody else would be more fun?"

"No," I said. "Of course not."

"Oh, really?" She drew out the word in a drawl. Then, harshly: "You think I'm stupid? You think I don't know you kids are mooning around missing Murdoch? Like he's so special! Like he's any fun at all! Like he could even compare to me. He knows nothing about parenting, not in the real world. He just has fantasy ideas about what it ought to be like."

"I never said anything about him and—"

She wasn't listening to me. "Or maybe you don't want fun at all!" She jerked the wheel to the left again.

And all at once, we were on the wrong side of the road, heading directly into oncoming traffic. Headlights glared straight into my eyes.

"Tell me you love me best," our mother said. Her voice was once more calm, and her hands on the wheel of the car were steady. "Convince me, Matthew."

I wanted to. I wanted to! But my throat had closed up. I couldn't speak—couldn't say what she wanted—couldn't—

The oncoming car swerved out of our way, honking madly, missing us by inches.

"Mom!" Callie yelled. "Mom, of course we love you—"

A horn blared, long and hard. Another oncoming car swerved out of our path, but there was another behind it—coming straight on—too close—

"I love you!" I screamed. "You're the best mother in the world!"

Our mother swerved back into our own lane, and laughed.

It took me a few seconds to realize we were safe again. Then I was vaguely amazed that I hadn't peed my pants. I put a hand on my seat belt.

Our mother said, breathlessly, "Oh, now *that* was fun. Wasn't that fun, guys? Sort of like a roller coaster." She laughed again. "Hey, for a second there, you know what? I really did think about it. I wondered what it would be like. Did you? Matt, how about you? Just for a sec? Didn't you want me to? What a way to go, too, in this great car. I love Jeeps, did you know?"

I didn't know. I didn't care. And no, I hadn't wanted to die.

It was important to respond to her, though. "We'll all know what it's like to die, one day," I said. "I can wait."

Nikki thought that was funny. "Right." Then she fell silent, thoughtful, for the remainder of the drive—during which she drove as carefully as if there were a police car on our tail.

I sat in the silence, in the passenger seat of the rented Jeep, my mouth dry and my hands shaking. I could feel Callie's terror from the backseat, but she said nothing either. There was nothing to say. At least you had slept through it all, Emmy.

I need to do something, I thought. *I need to get us out of this.*

13

FATHERS

It was then I remembered my father. My father and Callie's, Benjamin Walsh.

We didn't usually see much of him—not since he'd left Nikki. Emmy, that was way back when Nikki was (briefly) with your father. But Ben hadn't completely abandoned us. He sent a child-support check every month without fail, and he always included money for you, too.

In front of us, Nikki always called him "the nurse-boy," because he was a registered nurse and she thought that was a ridiculous job for a man. I called him Ben. Even when he was with us, I never said "Dad" or "Daddy," though Callie did. I'm not sure why. Maybe somewhere in me, even when I was small, I knew he couldn't be trusted when it mattered. He always deferred to Nikki.

Emmy, at that time, you had never even met Ben once,

and I'm not sure you even knew who we were talking about when we mentioned him, or even that Ben and Daddy and the nurse-boy were all the same person. I figured that it didn't matter what you thought about Ben. It just made me sad, that you didn't even have the idea of him—or of someone—as a father. Sometimes, when Callie said "Daddy," her voice lingered on the word. It's like a part of her forgot, or refused to believe, how little he mattered. How little he could do for us. How little he *was*.

I used to think that if Nikki was a tiger, then Ben was some animal that hides and scavenges; that scuttles about in fear. A giant mouse.

He'd left us, left me and Callie, just because he was told to. He was there one day, and then the next, he was slinking off with one old suitcase and a backpack, leaving behind lots of stuff he cared about, like his Australian work boots and a chess set that had belonged to his father.

I hid the chess set in the basement, so that Nikki wouldn't throw it out with everything else of his. But in the end it didn't matter that I'd kept it, because not only did Ben never ask about it—or anything else—but I found out that *I* didn't want to see it, either.

So, I despised Ben, okay? And yet . . .

And yet, Ben sent that money every month, and I knew from some of the kids at school that not all parents did that, even when the court told them to. Lots of divorced fathers got out of it somehow, but Ben sent $1,800 every month—$600 for me, $600 for Callie, and also $600 for you. And you weren't his child. No court or judge told him to do that.

Ben was not all that well-off, either. Registered nurses are in demand for jobs and make good money, but between what he paid out for the three of us and a lot of credit card debt that I later realized was from when he was married to Nikki, Ben was poor. He rented a single room for himself, in a house that belonged to other people. He said that was why we could never stay there with him, that he just didn't have room.

Now, he probably sent the money because he was frightened of Nikki. "I told the nurse-boy not even to think of trying to get out of it," our mother had said way back when. But it might not only have been that. It might also have been because Ben realized that you were a child, and you didn't ask to be born, but you existed and you needed stuff like any kid would. He might have done it because it was the right thing to do, and because he understood that in taking care of you, he helped take care of Callie and me, too.

That could be why. I would like to think that. That's the Ben I know today, anyway.

By the way, Emmy, I know what you're thinking as I talk about Ben. You're thinking about your own father. You're only nine years old as I write this, and I don't know how old you are as you read it. But when you're ready, I'll tell you what I know about your father. It isn't much. I remember his name, in case you want to try to find him. Callie knows it, too, and Aunt Bobbie.

The other thing I know is that he was rich. I still remember what happened the day Nikki realized your father had completely disappeared on her. Empty apartment, no forwarding address. It was pretty scary, and if you had been a physical object outside of her, something separate that could be hurt without hurting her, too— well. Thank God you weren't, that's all. And at least Callie and I were there for her to take it out on.

At that time, I didn't understand what exactly had happened between your father, our mother, and Ben. As I got older and could fit all the pieces together, I decided not to dwell on it. It didn't matter, I told Callie, if Nikki had thought your father was rich, a better bet than Ben— and more "fun"—and had tried to get him to marry her by becoming pregnant. It didn't matter. We had you, and we were glad to have you, even if it had worked out that we got you in some kind of weird Nikki-engineered exchange for Ben.

I doubt that Nikki tried to get Ben back after your father disappeared. I'd like to think he would have come back if she had asked him, and not just because he used to always do whatever Nikki said, but because of us kids. I know, however, that Nikki still thought she could do better than Ben. If not one rich guy, then another.

Not that Nikki was really a gold-digger. I actually don't think that about her. Take Murdoch, for example. Not that he was really rich, but he owned his house and all, and his own business. He was richer than us, richer than Ben. But if Nikki had really been thinking of bagging him, wouldn't she have controlled herself better?

Except maybe she couldn't. That's what I think now. She *couldn't* control herself.

Anyway. I bring Ben up because, on the day after the ride home from Six Flags during which Nikki nearly killed us all, I called him.

I told him I had to see him. Alone.

I had never asked him directly before to take us all away. To keep that $1,800 and use it so we could all be together, away from Nikki. I could help a lot, I thought. It wouldn't be like I was asking Ben to take care of three small children by himself. Callie and I took care of ourselves, and we would keep on taking care of you. It would be no trouble; it would be the same as ever, but away from Nikki.

We didn't need Murdoch, I told myself. Ben would do.

14
THINGS USUALLY WORK OUT OKAY

I had arranged to meet Ben on Tuesday afternoon, so at one thirty, coming out of American history class, I headed for the school library as if I were going to spend last period there. But when the bell rang, I slipped outside into the autumn sunlight. I could talk to Ben and still be home at the usual time.

It was only twenty minutes' walk from my school to the John F. Kennedy library and museum, next to the ocean. I sat down on a bench facing the water, with my back to the museum, and waited.

Ben wasn't late; I was early. I watched the crowds—tourists, students from UMass-Boston, and the usual runners and power walkers—all enjoying the wide sidewalks and ocean air of Columbia Point. I was just vaguely aware of my own mounting tension, and then I had an unexpected memory flash. A visual: the oncoming headlights of the car that had almost hit us on the highway the other night. The soundtrack: *Tell me you love me best.*

I would make Ben understand how serious this was. He couldn't know; he didn't see enough of us, or of her. And also, really, I hadn't fully understood it myself, before now. Not until we had those weeks with Murdoch had I truly seen how crazy our life was. When you're used to something, you don't really see it. But because of Murdoch, I could see now. It was no way to live. Because of Murdoch, I knew it should not go on. Because of Murdoch, it was now intolerable.

I would explain this so that Ben understood.

Then he was there, instantly recognizable in his faded green scrub pants, sneakers, and old denim jacket. I found myself on my feet, waving. And when Ben saw me and lifted his own arm in response, I was filled with a sudden wash of relief, almost of happiness.

"Hey," I said to him.

"Hey," Ben said. There was a little pause, and then he reached out, tentatively, and I found myself being hugged. I didn't hug back; I was too tense, and it only lasted a second.

"It's good to see you, Ben," I said.

He ducked his head a little and his pale yellow hair flopped onto his equally pale brow. "Yeah, me too. Listen, I'm sorry it's been a while. I've been working a lot of overtime. Doesn't mean I don't think about you guys."

I nodded. "Callie says hi," I said. It was a lie. Callie didn't know I'd called Ben or what I was going to ask him.

"How is she?" Ben asked.

"Okay. And Emmy's good, too—she's talking now. She's talking fine, when she wants to, and she's doing well in first grade, although she hates having to sit still so long every day. There's nothing wrong with Emmy."

"That's great," said Ben. Had his face stiffened when I mentioned you?

"She's a good kid," I said.

Ben nodded. He looked away, down at his feet.

For a few minutes we stood by the water, shifting from leg to leg, not speaking. I wished Ben would prompt me; ask me why I'd insisted on seeing him. Finally he gestured in the direction of the walkway. "Want to walk?"

"Sure."

It was better being in motion. I found a stone, a little chunk of mottled pink and gray granite, and began to kick it before me. "Listen, Ben," I said to the stone, "I need to tell you something." When he didn't say "Go ahead" or something like that, I looked over at his face, and after a second he looked back at me. That was when I saw that he was as afraid of this talk as I was.

And I knew then that he knew. Oh, not exactly what I was going to say, and not what Nikki had done in the

Jeep the other night. But he knew we weren't safe. He already knew that.

"Okay," he said carefully. "What is it?"

I went ahead anyway and told him about the incident in the car. Just the facts. What she'd said; what she'd done. That I thought it had been close. The whole time, I kicked my stone ahead of me.

When I finished, I reached down and picked up the stone and tossed it in one hand. That was when I dared look him in the face. He was crying. Hope pushed up again in me. He did care.

"We need to be somewhere safe, Ben," I said. "We need to be with you, not her. That would be better."

A pause. Then my father said, "It's complicated, Matt."

I stopped walking. "You know we shouldn't be there with her," I said. "You know it's not right. *She's* not right. She's sort of crazy, Ben."

It took him a few steps to realize I had stopped walking. He turned in the path, but he didn't move back toward me. Across two yards of concrete, his eyes fell from mine.

"It's complicated." His hands were plunged into the pockets of his jean jacket; his shoulders were raised and rigid. "Your mother has legal custody. I never fought her on that."

"You could now."

"It would be expensive . . . lawyers, you know. She'd fight back." He turned so he could pretend he was look-

68

ing out over the water. He had stopped crying, but made no attempt to wipe away the wetness. "And it would be difficult. Probably impossible. It would take months in court, maybe years. And even if it did work, which it probably wouldn't, she'd be angry the whole time. Angry at you guys. Angry at me. You know what that's like, when she's angry. There'd be more times like that one in the car."

I watched his profile as he talked to the Atlantic Ocean.

"I've thought about it before, Matt." Was that pleading in his voice? "For weeks after I moved out, I thought about whether I could get you and Callie. But there's nothing I can do. The courts favor the mother. And if she knew I wanted you, and that you wanted to come, that would make her even more determined to keep you. She wouldn't let go. Right?"

I didn't answer. I was listening again to what he'd just said. *Whether I could get you and Callie.*

"Emmy is littler than me and Callie," I said. "She can't take care of herself like we can. She's the one who really needs to be out of there."

"I could never get Emmy," Ben said. And now he did look at me, just for a second. "Even if somehow I could get legal custody of you and Callie, I would never be allowed to have Emmy. Nikki'd never let that happen. She'd make me take a blood test and show—well, you know. I don't have any right to Emmy."

"There's got to be a way," I said.

Ben just shook his head.

"What do we do, then?" The words burst out of me. "Hope for the best? Is that what you expect us to do? You think that's good enough?"

Ben said, "Maybe you're being a little dramatic. It'll work out. You'll be okay. She does love you. Things usually work out okay, if you just let them be."

I stared at him.

"She loves her kids." Ben's voice was stronger as he convinced himself. "In her own way. Our best bet is to let things be. You have to admit, she's a lot of fun sometimes. It's not all bad. Your aunt Bobbie's right downstairs. And I'm a phone call away. You can call me anytime, Matt. Just like you did this time. Do you have my work phone number?"

In my hand I could feel the stone. I threw it right at Ben's chest.

"Matt!"

I turned and walked away. Only after I had gone some distance did I realize that I had assumed he wouldn't actually let me go off like that. That he would follow me. Continue to talk.

But he hadn't. And when I finally turned to look back, he wasn't even there.

15

THE RULES OF SURVIVAL

After that, I stayed angry at Ben, but the feeling of desperation that I'd had after the car ride began to fade. My certainty that something horrible would happen if we continued living with Nikki started to seem silly as autumn drew on toward winter and nothing too out of the ordinary occurred. Nikki was Nikki, unpredictable, temperamental, and vicious, with weird little moments of generosity and laughter mixed in. But she always had been that way. We could cope, and we *would* cope, because we always had.

And also . . .

"Of course we have to stay with Emmy," Callie said, when eventually I told her about my talk with Ben. "If

Daddy couldn't take her, too, then what good would it be if he took us? She needs us. So, it's better this way. And he's right. We'll be okay. We'll absolutely be okay."

After a moment in which I fought two opposing impulses—the desire to agree with Callie, and the desire to scream at her to wake up, she added: "It's not Daddy's fault. He's doing what he can. And he's right that Mom probably wouldn't let us go, anyway. She'd fight and it would be awful, Matt."

I was ready to agree with that—it was true—when she repeated, "It's not Daddy's fault," and the words, *Yes, it is! It's his fault for not figuring out how to make things right! For not knowing how to stop her games!* almost ripped out of my mouth. Callie had talked too much, too fast—had been making too many excuses. Whether she knew it or not, she had doubts about her precious daddy. And blamed him. Oh, yes, she did.

But I managed to let it be. I don't know if she went on thinking about it, brooding about it, the way I did. We never discussed Ben's behavior again after that. To this day, we have not talked about it. But maybe it's meaningful, Emmy, that *she* is the one who lives with him now, while I chose to be with you and Aunt Bobbie.

Even I must admit that Ben was right to be afraid; right to try to keep his distance; and yes, right to leave when he did, how he did, without looking back. I blame him still for all of that, but beneath the lack of forgiveness and the lack of respect I feel for him, I understand why he did what he did. It was about self-preservation.

The human instinct for self-preservation is strong. I know, because mine pulls at me, too, like the needle on a compass. And everybody—I've been reading some philosophy—everybody seems to agree that the instinct and responsibility of all humans is to take care of themselves first. You have the right to self-defense. You have the right to survive, if you can.

But how come there don't seem to be any rules about when you ought to help others survive? Rules telling you when that's worth some risk to yourself? Callie and I were working so hard for you, Emmy, but as far as I could see, nobody else cared at all. For any of us.

16

PRAYER

On a Saturday in late October, Nikki came up behind me in the kitchen where I stood at the sink. I had started washing the huge pile of dishes, but I hadn't touched one in a couple of minutes. I was staring into space. I was thinking about Murdoch. Because of course, it wasn't only Ben I brooded about angrily that autumn. I thought of Murdoch much more often than I thought about Ben.

Thinking about Murdoch was a bad idea, though, and not just because it depressed and angered me. Nikki seemed able to sniff it out like a shark smelling blood.

I was wondering what Murdoch was doing right at that moment. Was he at home on East Tenth Street? It was only four blocks away. What would he say if I called him? How would it be if we tried to revert now to the old plan, Callie's old plan, of being friends with Murdoch? Would that be possible?

I jumped when Nikki spoke.

"Why are you so quiet, Matt? Don't tell me, I know. You're thinking about that loser again. Well, you know what? I think your precious Murdoch is gay, that's what I think. It all adds up. Didn't you notice the way he cooked? The way he always wanted things so clean? That's a sign. You never see a real man scrub a stove that way. You can have grease an inch thick before a real man would even notice. It's a good thing I got him away from you. I notice you doing more cleaning around here these days than you used to. Like those dishes. I didn't ask you to do them, did I?"

She paused, waiting for a reaction.

"No," I said. "I just noticed there were a lot of them. And none of Emmy's favorite dishes were clean."

"Hmm," Nikki said.

I tried to ignore her. I picked up a dish and gave it a swipe with the sponge.

"Matthew?" said my mother.

"What?"

"Did Murdoch ever try to molest you?"

"What?!" I turned and stared at her, my mouth gaping open.

She smiled. "Should I call Social Services and report him? I could do that, you know. I could report Murdoch for child abuse."

There was no way to reply to Nikki when she was like this. But at the same time, if I didn't reply, that might be the wrong thing, too.

"He never did anything to me," I said. "You know that." Instantly, I realized I would have done better to say nothing. She put a hand on my shoulder.

"Do I really know that? You have to understand," she said, sweetly now, "my first priority is protecting my kids."

"I'm fine," I said. I turned back to the dishes. "Nobody's done anything to me."

"I don't know," said Nikki. Something about her tone made me look at her again. A strange expression had filled her face; a kind of manic glee. "You don't seem happy these days. You seem worried and anxious, and I saw on TV that that can come from sexual abuse." She smiled again. "You might not even be aware. Sometimes kids repress these things."

"I would be aware," I said. I knew I should shut up, but I couldn't. "First, Murdoch's not gay. Second, even if he were, he'd never hurt a kid. You know that."

"No," Nikki said. "I don't know it. He's violent sometimes. Murdoch has a temper. He tries to keep it under control, but it's there. And you've changed, Matthew. You've gotten all sad and depressed. Something must have happened. I have my instincts, like any mother."

She sounded so reasonable. If I hadn't known her, I

would have believed her. A social worker would take her seriously.

"I think Murdoch is responsible for the change in you," said Nikki, accurately. "Maybe I'll report him." She squeezed my shoulder, as if comforting me, and then walked away toward her bedroom, humming to herself.

I picked up another dish with some vague idea that I would at least pretend to work—and it broke in two in my hands. The pieces fell into the dishwater. I wanted to pick them up, but I couldn't seem to move.

Now I would *have* to contact Murdoch. I would have to warn him about what Nikki might do. I would talk to him as soon as possible. I would call. Or, better, tell him in person. This wasn't the kind of thing you could say over the phone.

I concocted an immediate plan to go ring his doorbell that night, once Nikki went out. But I didn't. The reason was you, Emmy. You and a prayer.

That night, at bedtime, you knelt down by your bed in full view of Nikki, who had just read *Who Hops?* five times to you, with infinite patience and love. However, Nikki was also all dressed up to go out, and at this point, she was looking at her watch.

"You want to pray, Emmy-pie? Well, okay. Make it fast, though. Mommy's already late. She's going out."

So am I, I thought, but kept my face blank.

You bowed your head. You were silent a moment

while Nikki tapped her foot. Then you said, all in one breathless rush: "Dear God, please keep Murdoch safe and make him know I love him and miss him, thank you, God, amen."

My heart stopped.

You peeked up from your hands at Nikki, half scared, half delighted, all determined. And for the first time, I realized that one day, you might be a formidable woman. If you could stay safe now. Now and the next ten years.

I snatched you up one bare second before Nikki could get to you, turned, and raced to the bathroom, slamming the door shut behind us and locking it.

Nikki smashed her fist into the bathroom door. "You let me in there! Matthew! You let me in!"

Despite the way my heart was pounding, my voice was calm, as if I were responding to a question about whether, say, I wanted a glass of water. "Go out like you planned, Mom, and have a good time. You deserve a night out. I'll take care of Emmy. She'll still be here later, when you come home."

Silence. Then three hard bangs on the door. Slam. Slam. Slam.

You clung to me, your eyes wide and excited, absolutely aware of what was going on, and of your part in causing it. That meant we'd entered a whole new world. I'd worry about that later.

"Emmy will still be here later," I repeated through the door, in between bangs. "She. Will. Be. Here. Later."

I heard Callie's voice, outside the door, saying something to Nikki.

Then the banging stopped. From the other side of the door, Nikki spoke, as calmly as I had: "Okay. I'll be back later." And I heard her move away.

I didn't dare come out with you, though, until Callie told us Nikki had really gone out.

In silence, then, Callie and I put you to bed. You dropped right off to sleep like an angel, satisfied and exhausted by your work.

"What do you think she'll do to her?" I asked Callie tensely, after we retreated to the kitchen.

Callie shrugged. She stuffed her hands in her pockets. "I don't know. She might lock her in the hall closet for a few hours. She might not let her use the toilet. Or something else that she never did to me or you." She paused. "Or absolutely nothing at all."

I closed my eyes to rest them for a second. "We can't go on like this, Callie," I said.

"Oh? Do you have another idea?" said my sister.

I was silent.

Callie then said, apologetically: "Let's go watch TV, okay?"

"Okay," I said.

I thought: *Later, later, I'll go tell Murdoch. I have to, now.*

17

"TELLING"

Emmy, you have been living so safely in the suburbs with Aunt Bobbie and me these last years, with Callie not far away, and that's all you really remember nowadays. So, right about now, you might be wondering why I didn't "tell." Why I didn't go to a teacher at school, or to the police station, and report that we were scared to live with our mother and would somebody help us, please.

I suppose I could have done that, although I don't actually believe it would have worked. I think Nikki would have convinced an investigator that things were okay enough in our home. I decided that early on.

When I was in the fourth grade, a social worker came to talk to our class. She stood at the front of the room and explained to us that if someone hurt you, or touched you in a private place on your body, or if you were neglected, or if other things happened in your life that made you uncomfortable or scared, then you could just tell any adult at school about it. That adult—a teacher, an aide, the principal, it didn't matter who you told—would help instantly. That adult would talk to the other adults and they would contact state Social Services to investigate what you had said. Even if the person who had hurt you was in your own family, everything possible would be done to protect you.

"It's the law to protect children," the social worker had said. "It is also our sacred duty. We take it very seriously." She walked up and down the aisles of our classroom. She looked each one of us in the eye. "Tell someone," she said. "Always tell an adult here at school if you have a problem at home."

I listened to her carefully and with great interest. But I was not an abused or neglected child. I was a loved child, and so were my sisters. Nikki said so all the time. She did the things she did because she loved us.

Years later, when I began to understand that Nikki's form of love wasn't exactly the standard one, I still never really thought much about "telling" anyone. Once, I did try to imagine myself talking to a teacher. But the conversation in my head didn't get very far.

"Well, you see, our mother is weird and it's crazy living with her and her temper—uh, no, she doesn't hit us a lot. That's only happened a few times, and we never really got hurt. No, no broken bones. No bleeding. Sometimes there are men in and out—uh, no, nothing happens like what you're asking. We just have to hear what's going on, mostly. But the thing is, we worry a lot."

It didn't sound serious enough.

Callie and I knew a couple of kids from school who had had to go into foster care. Foster care didn't sound good, and it didn't sound safe. They often broke siblings up, we understood, and sent them to different families. And then, in the end, the kids were just sent home again after the parents promised to do better, or had taken some parenting class or something like that.

We were better off just sticking it out with Nikki.

And you know what? I still think that, even now. I think that if Callie or I had told the authorities, even if we were taken seriously, even if there was an investigation as a result, it would just have been a detour. Our fate was our fate.

18

CALLIE'S PLAN

Callie and I stayed up that Saturday night, wanting to be awake when Nikki came home—she didn't, by the way, until well into the morning—in case she was still mad at you about the prayer for Murdoch. And at the time we thought it was just as likely that she would *not* still be angry. She did have the capacity to forgive and forget completely. Or she could be distracted by other things— she might come home with a man, for example. Or a new pair of pants. But also, she could wait, sometimes, until you were sure she had forgotten whatever it was you had done. And then you would discover that she had *not* forgotten.

You just never knew.

We flung ourselves on the rug in front of the TV and channel-surfed until Callie found a movie called *Pleasant-*

ville that she wanted to watch. It was about a brother and sister who are magically transported into the world of a black-and-white television show from the 1950s, where everything is nice and predictable and utterly good, and there's nothing tricky to deal with like sex or imagination or fear. But the girl sets out to destroy Pleasantville because she doesn't like things to be safe. She wants them messy and colorful and passionate and alive. The movie meant this to be a good thing, but I didn't like it. Once I realized where the movie was going, I grabbed the remote control and changed the channel to a movie about college kids.

"You don't mind, do you?" I asked Callie.

"No." But my sister was clearly less interested in this movie than in the Pleasantville one. I felt her eyes on me.

"Matt, listen. Why did Emmy say what she did tonight?"

"You mean about Murdoch?"

"Yeah."

"I guess she still thinks about him," I said. "And misses him."

"Right," Callie said patiently. "But I meant, why did she come out and say it to Mom? Why didn't she know better?"

"She did it on purpose. I could tell."

"She ought to know better!"

"She does," I said. "She decided to do it anyway."

84

Callie picked up the remote from where it lay on the carpet between us. She switched the TV back to *Pleasantville,* where the girl was causing people to see things in color. She was like an infection, that girl. I tried to get the remote back, but Callie put it under her stomach.

"That's a problem," she said.

"Yeah," I said. "I'll talk to her."

"You know what it is?" Callie said thoughtfully. "It's that she feels safe."

"What are you talking about?"

"Emmy feels safe. She knew we would protect her from Mom, and so she felt like she could say whatever she wanted. Take the risk." She paused. "And as long as she feels safe, she might keep on doing stuff like that."

"What exactly are you trying to say?" I sat up and turned my back to the movie. "That we shouldn't protect Emmy?"

Callie kept staring at the TV. "No."

"That's what it sounded like you were saying."

"I'm just thinking things out." Callie's voice was flat. "Emmy feeling safe is dangerous. For her. For us. It's just a fact, Matt. I never imagined she would feel safe." She added: "*I* never have."

I turned away from Callie. Of course it was better, safer, for Emmy, with both of us older and on the watch. I had only been one and a half when Callie was born. I had done my best.

On the television, the brother, who had loved Pleasantville before, was becoming convinced that his sister was right after all. Color and life were better, even if they came with pain and death attached. Wow, thanks for the explanation, Hollywood. I said, "I'm glad that Emmy feels safe. It means we're doing a good job."

"Maybe. But we're just doing what we always did." A pause. "I don't think it's only about us."

I saw where she was going. "Murdoch," I said. "You're saying that Emmy feels safe because of Murdoch. Even though he's gone."

Callie's hands gripped each other. "Look. I'm not sure how to say this. But Matt, it's time to stop dreaming. It's time to live in the real world. All of us, I mean. Emmy. You." A pause. "And me."

Was that an admission? It didn't matter. I said, "I do live in the real world."

"You know what I'm trying to say," said Callie softly.

I did. I hoped she wouldn't say it out loud, but she did. It didn't matter that her voice stayed soft.

"Matt, it's all over. He's gone."

"I know that," I said.

"No, you don't. You're still hoping, like Emmy. But you know what? Murdoch's not some superhero who's going to swoop in and change everything. That dream is over. Our life is what it is. Don't you see? It's getting dangerous to go on dreaming that it's going to be different."

"Because of what Emmy said tonight."

"That's not the only thing," said Callie, even more

softly. And then I did turn to look at her. In an instant I knew.

I said, "You heard Nikki this afternoon. You heard what she was threatening about Murdoch."

Callie nodded.

I shrugged. "I'll warn him," I said.

"No," said Callie. "You have to forget him. Not pretend to. Really forget. We have to get on with our lives as they are. Listen, Matt. Think for a minute. Even when you went to talk to Daddy, you were really thinking about Murdoch. You were trying to make Ben be Murdoch."

"No," I said. "That's not true."

"It is."

"No," I said again. But in fact, she was right that I'd had superhero fantasies, father fantasies . . .

"I'm sorry," Callie was saying. "Matt, I'm so sorry. I wish it had all come true. But it didn't. Okay? We agree?"

I nodded. "Yes."

"We can get back to normal here if we try. That's what we need to do. We need to get back to thinking and feeling exactly the way we did before. It's the *only* way to reassure Mom."

"But how are we supposed to do that?" I said. "Program ourselves to forget? I can't. Emmy can't."

"We just pretend."

"I've been pretending."

"We have to do a good job at it. A great job."

I was silent.

"Will you try, Matt? We can't mention him or even think of him. We have to erase him from our memories. He has to be dead to us. That time, last summer—it never happened. It was just like the summer before." Callie got right in my face. "Emmy's only little, Matt. Just six. If we help her to forget, she will."

"What if she doesn't?"

"She will if we show her how," said Callie. And then she added, "And so will you. In time, we'll all forget." She waited.

I didn't believe I would. I also didn't believe we could go back in time. But Callie was right that you, Emmy, couldn't be allowed to goad Nikki. "Okay," I said.

19
DEMONS

What neither Callie nor I knew that night, as we talked about trying to go back in time in our relationship with Nikki, was that things were changing in our mother—just as you, Callie, and I had changed. I believe it had to do with Murdoch, Murdoch as kind of a catalyzing experience in our lives, the chemical ingredient that made an already poisonous compound unstable as well. I might be wrong; it might simply have been time itself that destabilized us so sharply and so permanently. Whatever it was, the end result was the same: No amount of pretending could take us back to the way we were before.

The change in Nikki over that winter . . . I'm trying to find a way to describe it.

Okay. Emmy, this is what I think: Demons are real. Since I'm not religious, I think of them as metaphors for the evil desires and impulses all humans have. A religious person can think of them as separate evil beings that can possess you. Either way, I believe they exist, lurking patiently around and in us, whispering their twisted points of view, ever alert for an opportunity. The sudden chink in your armor when you're tired, frightened, or angry. The invitation you issue in that moment of vulnerability.

Come inside me. Tell me what to do.

I believe that I could and should have known about the demons that were on the borderline of ruling our mother. I had actually seen something in her eyes and felt some force in the air around her for many years. The demons are unmistakable even when you don't have a name for them. So, I knew. And yet, I didn't.

My mistake was that I thought the demons already ruled her. I thought they were already in control. But I know now that, in her own strange way, she had been doing her best all those years, the years before Murdoch, to hold them at bay. They had her ear, but not her soul.

Now, I am not saying that she fought her demons in the years before Murdoch. Nikki played with them before. But she was not ruled by them before Murdoch and they did not own her.

And then—at some point, right around this time, maybe even the very night I promised Callie that I would try to forget Murdoch—at some point right around that very night, our mother invited the demons into her soul.

I really believe that this was what happened. The lock was opened. The key was thrown away.

Come inside me. Tell me how to get what I want.

I believe that she thought the demons would help her win back the love and dependence of her children from the thief who had stolen them. I believe she chose this route on the night that you prayed for Murdoch in order to spite her.

One more thing. On that night I, too, was trying to think of some way to restabilize our lives. Callie had her own idea, as I've already described. And my idea involving Ben had already been shot down.

Despite my promise, my mind kept turning back to Murdoch. The man I'd seen in the Cumberland Farms, and the man we'd gotten to know since. That man wouldn't feel right, abandoning kids in trouble. Real trouble. He was trying to do just that, of course, but what if . . .

What if I put some pressure on him?

20
CHURCH

Nikki didn't come home that night, and by the next morning, when she did, she had a new man with her. He was the first man she'd brought home since Murdoch. She herded him into the kitchen, where we were sitting around the table pretending to eat cereal.

A half hour before, Callie and I had begun trying to have our talk with you, Emmy. We wanted you to agree to a new family rule: Never, ever mention Murdoch's name, at least not in front of Nikki, but preferably never.

You had not wanted to promise. You folded your arms and stuck out your lower lip. "You can't make me!" You were the defiant, powerful, and self-confident Emmy of the previous night, praying for Murdoch, defying Nikki.

Callie wheedled. I pleaded. Callie threatened. I

bribed. I was thinking we were making progress—you sighed and lowered your head—when we heard the front door and footsteps on the stairs. Nikki's laughter. A man's voice.

We barely had time to throw together a just-the-kids-having-breakfast scene. You cooperated with that, at least. You were in your booster seat at the table, chomping on Froot Loops, when Nikki came in, pulling a large man behind her by the hand. The man was balding and ponytailed and very, very big. He wore an old leather jacket and frayed jeans, and had a big collection of keys clinking at his side. He could barely tear his hopeful, avid eyes away from Nikki.

"This is Rob," Nikki said carelessly to us. "My kids," she said to him. She didn't bother telling him our names. He wouldn't know it, but that meant he wasn't going to be around for long. I was relieved.

"Hi, Mom," said Callie. She threw me a quick look, but I didn't need her reminder.

"Hi," I said. I couldn't quite manage to smile at Nikki, but I said, "Want me to make coffee?"

"Sure," said Nikki. "Thanks, hon." Then she looked at you, Emmy.

You picked up a yellow Froot Loop, stuck out your tongue, delicately placed the Froot Loop on it, and waggled it. With your other hand, you picked up your Minnie Mouse mug. I saw Nikki's gaze travel to it, and I remembered Murdoch had bought it for you.

It would have to be thrown out. You were too old for it anyway, really.

"Say hi, Emmy," said Callie. I could feel her tension.

You took your time chewing and swallowing the Froot Loop. Then: "Hi, Emmy," you parroted.

Nikki decided to laugh, but it was a short bark that might possibly have convinced Rob she was amused, but would fool no one else, including you. "Tell me when the coffee's ready," Nikki said to me. She took Rob's hand and guided him out of the room. We heard her bedroom door close, but not before we also heard Rob say: *I just can't believe my luck.*

I turned on the radio and punched the tune button at random. Church music came on—an organ. It was deep and sonorous and filled the room.

I got busy making Nikki's coffee at the counter. She liked it weak, with milk. I didn't know how Rob liked his coffee. So, what was I supposed to do, go knock on the door and ask? Would I have done that six months or a year ago, before Murdoch? What exactly did it mean to act normal, the way Callie thought we should?

The organ music from the radio swelled in the background.

You were now crunching Froot Loops with vigor, using your hands to eat. Murdoch would have insisted on you using a spoon. Defiantly, I found one and handed it to you. You looked at it, at me, and then condescended to use it.

I cleared my throat. "Well, what should we do today?" I asked my sisters. "Go on over to Castle Island? Emmy, you can go on the swings. I don't think it'll be too cold if we keep moving."

Callie didn't look up from her own cereal. She was stirring it intently, but it didn't look like she'd actually eaten any. She replied immediately. "I think we should get dressed and go to church. Like, right now. How about that one over on East Broadway? I'm pretty sure they have a Mass at nine o'clock or nine thirty or something like that."

"What?" We hardly ever went to church.

Callie stirred her cereal faster. "The music made me think of it. Why not, Matt?" She stopped stirring and shrugged. "It'll get us out of the house. They're open on Sunday morning. And Emmy likes praying. Well, she can pray at church."

If there was an edge to Callie's voice, you didn't pick up on it. You looked interested. "I can pray at church?"

"Yes," I said. "You can. That would be okay."

Callie looked up at last and our eyes met. I nodded at her. She bit her lip. "I'll go get stuff we can wear," she said. "I don't want Emmy having to change back there in our bedroom . . . with—with him here. We can take her downstairs and change in the hall outside Aunt Bobbie's."

I nodded again.

Callie disappeared.

95

The organ music came to an end. The radio announced: "That was Cantata 147, 'Jesu, Joy of Man's Desiring,' by Johann Sebastian Bach, played by the Academy of St. Martin-in-the-Fields, conducted by David Willcocks. This is National Public Radio. Here at WBUR, our new fiscal year begins in just ten days . . . "

I finished making the coffee. I had decided to prepare Rob's just the same as Nikki's. I squared my shoulders. I would take the two mugs to her door. I would do it now.

I turned with the mugs just as Callie reappeared in the doorway, her arms filled with clothes that she had gathered rapidly, too rapidly. In the pile, I could see your blue summer dress with the yellow ducks on it, and a white dress shirt for me that I was pretty sure no longer fit. Callie took one step into the kitchen and dumped the stuff onto the table, the sleeve of my dress shirt flying perilously close to her abandoned cereal bowl. Her cheeks were red, as if she'd been running.

And then Nikki appeared in the doorway right behind Callie. She was dressed, but barely, in her green and red silk robe with the dragon on the back. At least I didn't have to go into her bedroom. I managed to smile at her. I walked across the kitchen so I could hand her the mugs.

" . . . that's why we count on the support of loyal listeners like you . . ."

"Your coffee, Mom," I said, and then I saw the tiny bit of leftover white powder just beside her right nostril.

I don't think my face changed, but somehow my gaze tangled with hers and she read my mind as easily as a monkey peels a banana. She put her right hand up to her nose, captured the bit of powder on her fingertip, put it to her nostril, and sniffed. She stared into my eyes the whole time.

" . . . and for every donation of a hundred and twenty dollars that you make in the next hour, your money will be matched . . . "

I turned back to the counter, put one mug down very precisely, and snapped the radio off. Then I picked the mug back up. "Coffee?" I said.

Nikki waved away the mugs with one hand. She gestured at the pile of clothes on the kitchen table. "What's all this?"

"Well," said Callie brightly, "we're getting dressed to go to church this morning."

"To pray," you said, smiling a sly smile.

Nikki narrowed her eyes at you. Then her gaze traveled to Callie and me in turn.

And then she threw back her head and laughed. The laugh came out full and long and generous.

"Rob!" Nikki called. "Hey, Rob, get this! My kids are getting ready for church!"

There was no reply from the bedroom, but that didn't appear to bother Nikki. She was looking at the clothes again, and then from the pile back to me. A serious look of assessment came over her face. "Matt, you'll need a different shirt. This one won't fit you anymore. You should throw it out."

"I will." I took the shirt from her.

"Good," she said briskly. "Try the left side of your closet. I think there's a long-sleeved blue button-down that will fit. I bought it for you at Marshalls last year, and it was big then. Wear it with chinos, not jeans." Her gaze moved on. "Callie, honey, you shouldn't wear pants to church. It's not right. Why don't you just wear your plaid school skirt? With a cardigan." She had fished Callie's green jeans and black sweater off of the table. "Put these back."

Callie took them. "Okay. Great. Thanks." She didn't look at me, or me at her, but we didn't need to do that to share our relief.

Nikki had now picked up your summery dress, the last thing on the table, and was shaking her head.

"I'll find something else for Emmy, too, Mom," I said. "I know she can't wear that. It's not warm enough."

"Oh, no," said Nikki easily. She handed the dress to me. "Just put it away. You don't need to find another one. You two are going, but not Emmy. She's been bad, so I'll just keep her with me and Rob today. After all, she's already shown us that she can pray perfectly well without church."

While we gaped at her, she turned back to the table and picked up your Minnie Mouse mug. "Wash this for me, Matt, and put my coffee in it."

21
RIGHT AFTERWARD

"It's not so bad," I said uncertainly to Callie, as we lingered on the sidewalk in front of our house. With the front door of the house shut behind us, we could no longer hear your furious screams. *I wanna go to church! Matt, take me! Callie! I want to go pray for Murdoch! You said I could!* "Maybe it'll teach Emmy not to—not to . . . "

Callie gave me a look. "You want her taught things?"

I had a sudden vision of our mother, upstairs in her dragon robe, and of that huge man she'd brought home. "Shut up," I said sharply. "Shut up. This was your idea— your stupid idea. I thought we were going to pretend things were the way they were before. Well, huh? Huh? We don't usually go to church."

She did shut up. I crossed my arms and hunched my shoulders. Callie had her coat, but I hadn't remembered my jacket, and it was a chilly, damp autumn day. We didn't move from our chosen spot in front of the house, looking up at it from time to time even though we were too close to even see the third-floor bay window of our apartment. We certainly could not see inside.

There had barely been time to scramble into the clothes Nikki had picked out for us before we felt her hands at our backs, literally pushing. And then the apartment door slammed behind us, the dead bolt clicked audibly into place on the other side, and we were left on the inner stairs, with nothing to do but step down, down, down. Past Aunt Bobbie's second-floor apartment, where the television blared. Past the first-floor apartment, where the college students probably still slept. With each step, your cries faded, until we closed the front door behind us.

"How long is church?" I asked eventually.

"I don't know. An hour?"

"That's not long."

"No."

Still, we didn't move. Across the street, tiny old Mrs. Hennigan was kneeling on her stoop, completely absorbed with stuffing rags into a pair of jeans and a shirt. Eventually, she sat the headless scarecrow carefully on a child's plastic chair, positioned a large pumpkin head on its lap, and competently hammered the scarecrow's gloved hands to the pumpkin head.

"I forgot my jacket," I said to Callie.

"Do you want to go back for it?"

"Should I?"

"You could. She'll be mad. But you could."

We stood there. I was so cold.

"Well?" Callie said.

"I'll live without it," I said. "Let's go to church. We can come back right after and see if she'll let us in then. It's only an hour."

"Yes." Callie didn't move, though. "I wonder—maybe we could go back in and ask Aunt Bobbie . . ."

"Ask her what?"

"Just to keep an eye out."

I sneered. "We'll do better praying."

Callie nodded. Listen, Emmy: Aunt Bobbie wasn't Aunt Bobbie then, like she is now. We didn't think she would help us. Actually, then, I don't think she would have.

And so we went to church, the big Catholic one on Broadway, and when we came back, Nikki had taken you and—with that guy Rob, too, for all we knew—disappeared.

And then we did go to see Aunt Bobbie, who was indeed no real help. "Well, you know how Nikki is. She'll be back tonight. Or, worst case, in a day or two. I suppose you could have dinner here. Yes! Why don't we plan on that? I'll get us one of those big buckets of chicken, with the biscuits and everything." She paused, thoughtful, and then added, "Maybe two buckets."

22

AUNT BOBBIE

On the rare occasions when I have had to tell a version of my life story to outsiders, I move Aunt Bobbie up front and center. "My little sister Emmy and I live with our aunt, Roberta O'Grady. We have for years now. She's our legal guardian."

And if one day I meet a girl, I will take her home to meet Aunt Bobbie. I will explain how Aunt Bobbie took us in and sort of saved our lives. And Aunt Bobbie will glow, the way she does when you introduce her casually to your friends from school: *Aunt Bobbie's my aunt, but she's also my mother.* I've heard you say just that, Emmy.

Sometimes, I look at this new Aunt Bobbie, the one who plans college applications with me, who cheers herself hoarse at Callie's field hockey games, and who reviews your homework and braids your hair. She looks the same as ever—a plainer, inflated version of Nikki. But that other Aunt Bobbie heard just about everything her sister said and did, ten feet above her head, and she never said a word to interfere or even to offer us comfort. Then she became this new person. Just like that.

What Murdoch says about Aunt Bobbie's change is: "Remember that quote: 'Some are born great, some achieve greatness, and some have greatness thrust upon them.'"

"Uh, but Aunt Bobbie had motherhood thrust upon her."

"No. Greatness. Bobbie didn't know she was strong—stronger than her sister." He never uses Nikki's name nowadays. Just "your mother" or "her sister." "She didn't know she had ideals and principles, because she'd buried them so deep."

"But she ignored so much, for so long. How come suddenly—"

"One day, she took that first step to get involved. It felt right to her, so that led to more. It's simple."

This is what Aunt Bobbie says about the change—I've heard her, when she talks to a few friends of hers:

"Well, maybe I should have seen my sister's life more clearly earlier. Seen that she was out of control and it wasn't good for the kids. I look back, and I should have known. I guess I didn't let myself. But, well, there's no sense crying over it now. What's done is done. And once I fully understood the situation, I acted. I give myself credit for that. And I have to say, I have never had a moment of regret.

"No, it's really not such a big responsibility as all that. Matt was already almost grown up, and Emmy, well, it's just not a burden. I thought I was going to spend my whole life alone, and look: I'm a mother! And they're great kids, no trouble at all, nothing like Nikki. And their father's around, too. He helps a lot these days. Callie—that's the older sister—she decided to live with him. The way I see it, I have a lot to be grateful for.

"So, listen, my Em is going to be in the Christmas pageant at St. Anne's. She's one of the three wise men. They're selling tickets here at the grocery next week, if you're interested in bringing your niece. One tip, though. They've been using the same costumes for the last twenty years. I don't think they've ever been washed, so don't sit in the first few rows."

That's Aunt Bobbie. A mystery.

23
FIRST BLOOD

Nikki did eventually come back with you, just as Aunt Bobbie had predicted. The new man, Rob, was not with you—I knew that immediately, from the sounds on the stairs that night at 10:32. Only two sets of feet, one light—yours—the other the unmistakable clomp of Nikki's heels. Then her voice, only slightly annoyed, talking to you. "Okay, okay, we're home, just like you wanted all day. Are you happy now?"

Nikki strode into the apartment, hauling you by one hand. The strong smell of Chinese food came in with you; Nikki was holding a big brown paper bag. "Put the little crybaby to bed, will you?" she said to Callie, but her tone was still mild, and a smile was playing around her mouth and her eyes. Wherever she had been, whatever she had been doing—she had had a good time.

Your mouth was set tight. And you had been crying—your eyes were reddened—but that was okay, I thought, because you were all right somehow. I could see at once, from the mutinous way you had hunched your shoulders, that your spirit was intact. Spurning Callie's outstretched hand, you marched to our bedroom, throwing your coat on the living room floor as you went. "*Nobody* put me to bed!" You slammed the bedroom door behind you.

"Then stay there!" Nikki yelled after you. "Little brat! I should never have had you, anyway!"

I watched Nikki carefully, but your slammed door didn't affect her good humor. A second later, she was tossing her hair and rolling her eyes at Callie and me. "What a little pain in the ass she can be, huh? All day, *I wanna go home, I wanna go home, I wanna go home.*"

I decided to risk that good humor. "So, where'd you go?"

"First, to Rob's. Then just to the mall." Nikki shrugged. I waited to see if more information would be forthcoming, but it wasn't. Nikki put the bag of Chinese takeout on the counter and opened it. She insisted we all sit down at the table and have a feast. "I'm ravenous! I got Emmy an ice cream at the mall, but I haven't eaten since morning. And I wanted to make it up to you, since you two missed dinner."

"No, we didn't," Callie said. I wished she would watch her tone; she sounded almost belligerent. "Aunt Bobbie invited us for dinner. But if she hadn't, I'd have made something. Or Matt would have."

Nikki shrugged, undisturbed. This was a good mood for the record books. She gestured firmly to us to sit at the table, and we did, although Callie pushed her plate away empty. "Bobbie served you dinner? She actually shared her food?" She laughed, her hands deftly placing five cartons of Chinese food onto the table, followed by utensils. Then she seated herself. "So, do tell, what'd you eat there, frozen chocolate cake? A bowl of potato chips?"

"Chicken," I said.

"Kentucky Fried," Nikki guessed instantly, correctly. "And Bobbie ate all the biscuits, right? Slathered in butter? My sister is such a freak. How much do you suppose she weighs?" She was looking at Callie now, who shrugged and didn't answer. "Two hundred thirty?"

This was an old game of Nikki's, making fun of Aunt Bobbie. There were lots of ways to do it; Bobbie's weight was only the most popular. We had always participated before. There was no reason—then—to love Aunt Bobbie or to try to understand why it was she wanted and needed so much food, or to speculate about what it might have been like for her, growing up as the younger sister to the pretty, popular, selfish, headstrong, and maybe even crazy Nikki—and with a dead mother and a gambling father, too.

So, remembering my promise to Callie—go back to

normal—I joined in. "Two fifty, I bet," I said. "She ate all the biscuits except for the two that Callie and I ate, and I counted four pieces of chicken on her plate. Plus, she bought a whole spare bucket of chicken that she's probably eating right now." I tipped my head downward. Aunt Bobbie's kitchen was right under ours.

"God!" Nikki said. "Sick!" Her eyes were bright with enjoyment, with her fork paused midway between her plate of beef with broccoli and her mouth. Then she stabbed a piece of broccoli and shook her head, smiling generously at Callie. "Well, girl, maybe you were right, then. About not eating more now. I wouldn't want you to end up like my sister. You don't have to eat anything else now. Just keeping me company like this, that's enough. Hanging out with my kids is a good enough time for me. Actually, I should have gotten brown rice, and not this pork fried stuff. It would've been healthier. I'll remember that next time."

"Oh, I like pork fried rice," I put in. "It's a treat. And this way, we can have lots of leftovers. I love leftovers."

"Unless," lilted Nikki, "we send them on down to Bobbie!"

I laughed with her. I am ashamed to say that it wasn't hard to do. Callie's right, I thought, Callie's right. We can do this. I can do this. Normal, normal, normal. Normal for us.

And then I realized that Callie wasn't laughing. That she hadn't said a word since we sat down. I looked at her.

She had reached for one of the cartons and was spooning fried rice onto her plate. A lot of fried rice, I saw with astonishment. While Nikki and I watched, she added just as much of the beef with broccoli, cashew shrimp, and chicken chow mein, until her plate was heaped high.

"I thought you already ate," Nikki said dryly. She still sounded fine. Calm. Mildly interested. What was she *on*? Whatever it was, I liked it; she was nowhere near an explosion. And she was watching Callie as carefully as I was, but with an expression that wasn't her usual cat-at-the-mouse-hole. This was one I didn't recognize. There was a little frown of concern in the middle of her forehead. But, at the same time, she was also sort of smiling.

"I know I said that." Callie's head was down over her plate. Her fork was moving rapidly between it and her mouth. "I'm just suddenly very hungry. It's weird."

For a few moments we both continued to watch her, and then—

"Callie?" Nikki asked kindly. "Are you getting your period?"

It was like a bomb thrown into the room. I nearly choked on my egg roll. I felt myself blush.

"Mom!" Callie's head came up and for a split second she glared toward me. Then her face went right down again. She muttered, "I don't, yet." And then, her voice skittering high, she added: "God, don't you even *know* that? What kind of a mother *are* you?"

109

I froze—Callie, no!

But Nikki only smiled. And then, suddenly, she was the other Nikki, the wonderful Nikki. Emmy, I haven't told you much about this side of her, because—well, I don't want to remember it. But sometimes, sometimes, she was this mother, too.

She got up from the table. She went over to Callie's chair, knelt beside her, and touched Callie's cheek gently. "Sweet girl," she said, "I'm the kind of mother that knows everything she needs to know. Baby, listen to me. This happens to every woman. You are about to be thirteen. I was twelve. It's natural."

"That is so not what's going on with me right now!" Callie wailed.

"Don't be afraid, baby girl. Don't be afraid. It's a beautiful thing." She held out her arms.

And Callie went into them and sobbed. Nikki stroked her hair. She looked across at me and said, "Go keep Emmy company for a little while, would you, Matthew? Thanks, dear."

I was more than glad to leave.

But as I was getting up, the phone rang. It was well after eleven o'clock, but late calls were a fact of life at our house. Nikki waved an imperious hand toward Callie, indicating she was to shut up with the sobs now. Callie, thankfully, wasn't so far gone that she didn't obey. Then Nikki answered the phone, smiling.

"Rob," she said warmly. "There you are. I've been

waiting to hear from you. So, did you take care of that little thing for me like you promised? Remember, you also promised to tell me every little detail. Actually, you might need to come over here and tell me in person . . . What did you say?"

Several seconds ticked by. The warm, amused, happy expression on Nikki's face faded and was replaced by pure rage. We'd seen this before, many times. Except we hadn't. Not quite like this. I already explained about the demons, so I won't waste any more time on it, except to say that they were suddenly there. They were inside her.

Eventually, Nikki spoke again. Her eyes were on us, on Callie and me across the kitchen table from her, but she wasn't seeing us at all. She was communing with her demons. And Rob.

"What?" she said to Rob. "What?! You absolute loser, are you trying to tell me that Murdoch beat *you* up?"

24

THE NEIGHBOR

I went looking for Murdoch as soon as I could the next morning.

Nikki had gone on a rampage when she'd gotten off the phone the night before, screaming, hurling the cartons of Chinese food at the walls, and ranting about what had happened. "Get out of here! Get out of here!" she'd yelled at Callie and me, and we'd barricaded ourselves in the bedroom, which was dim with only your night-light on, while our mother raged.

"I'll make him pay! He'll pay!"

It went on for hours. At one point, sometime near two in the morning, Rob was actually there, trying to explain himself. Murdoch couldn't have hurt Rob very much, I thought, if Rob could come over—drag himself up the steep flights of stairs. But of course I couldn't see him.

The three of us eavesdropped instead. It was hard to hear Rob, but Nikki's voice was as audible as a bullhorn. I easily put the whole story together. There wasn't a lot to it, actually.

Emmy, there was no possible way to protect you from hearing that our mother had hooked up with and seduced a stranger, a large man, intending to get him to do physical harm to her ex-boyfriend. And there was also no way to prevent you from understanding what you heard. You were six years old by then, and the fact that you had taken your time to speak didn't mean you weren't smart. And also, I figure you knew.

I figure you heard the whole plan during that day that you were with Nikki and Rob. I figure that was your punishment for praying for Murdoch: being forced to listen to plans to hurt him. Maybe being told that you were the reason it was happening.

It was just the kind of thing Nikki would do.

Your eyes were wide in the dimness as you listened. Then they got narrow. What you were thinking, I don't know.

"I'll go find Murdoch tomorrow," I said. I hunched down on the floor next to you and whispered. To you, not to Callie, although Callie was listening, too, of course. "I'll make sure Murdoch's okay."

"Murdoch is fine," you said matter-of-factly. "Can't you hear? That other man, he's the one who's hurt." There was great satisfaction in your voice, even though it was as low as mine. I glanced at Callie to see if she heard it, too, and to see what she thought. But she was huddled against the wall with her knees drawn up in front of her, rocking herself. And suddenly she said, "I don't care, I've got to go," and at the next burst of screaming from Nikki, Callie thrust herself up from the floor and was at the door, pushing away the bureau I'd moved in front of it. I was afraid of her being out there, but I made no move to stop her. A while later, Callie came safely back. She flung herself onto her mattress and curled into a little ball, ignoring you and me and the screaming coming from Nikki in the living room.

I pushed the bureau back against the door. I picked you up and put you to bed, and then crawled into mine, and the three of us stayed awake the rest of the night, listening in the dimness until Nikki finally wound herself down, half an hour or so before dawn.

Not long after that, when Nikki had finally quieted down, I told you and Callie that we all were going to school that day like normal. Yes, we were all tired. But so what? School was our job, I said. I knew, though, that I was lying. I didn't intend to wait until after school to try to find Murdoch. Once I had taken you to school, I went straight to Murdoch's house on East Tenth Street.

Murdoch didn't answer his doorbell when I rang, even though I pressed it repeatedly for ten whole minutes. But his extended cab Toyota truck was sitting in front of his house, with its windshield and side windows smashed.

I stopped and stared at it. The windows weren't broken, only spiderwebbed with cracks—I guessed that the glass was that safety stuff. But they had been comprehensively destroyed. I stepped closer to look, aware that I was finding it a little hard to breathe.

A baseball bat, I guessed, or something similar, had caused this.

No. Rob had caused this.

No again. Nikki had caused this. Our mother had caused this.

I wondered: Had Murdoch been in his truck, or getting out of it, when Rob went after him? How was Murdoch? What had happened, when, how? I had to know.

There was a big sign on the driver's seat. It said: *Sam, please call me before you tow the truck. Thanks.*

I could telephone Murdoch, too, I thought. I had the cell phone he'd given me, with lots of time still left on it because I used it so rarely, to save the minutes for emergencies. I didn't want to talk to him on the phone, though. I wanted to just find him. I wanted to see him. I wanted—

My eyes fell on the door of the house next to Murdoch's. It was attached to his, sharing the whole inner wall, and I knew the name—I groped for it—of the woman who lived in the first-floor condo. Julie Lindemann. That was it. I knew her car, too—that was it over there, across the street, a new white Beetle convertible. Its presence meant she hadn't left for work yet. She and Murdoch had some joke about how she was a big gas-waster because she could take the bus to work but never did.

I sat down on the stoop of Murdoch's house, which was also the stoop of Julie's house, and waited, and after about half an hour, Julie let herself out of the door right next to me. I stood up and said her name, and she jumped about two feet in the air, dropping her keys.

"Oh my God, you scared me!"

"I'm sorry. I'm Matthew Walsh. Do you remember me? I'm a friend of Murdoch's."

I saw that she did remember me. Her eyes looked a little wary, though, and I wondered if Murdoch had said anything to her about us, about our mother. She bent down to pick up her keys, but I got to them first and handed them to her.

"Thanks," she said.

I nodded toward Murdoch's wrecked truck. "What happened?"

"I don't know," Julie said. But I could tell that she wasn't shocked to see the smashed windows. I could tell from her expression as she glanced at the truck that she'd already seen them—maybe even last night, when it happened. Her front window was only twenty feet from where the truck was parked. She might have seen the whole thing. If she'd been home, she must have heard it. That whole end of the street must have heard it.

"Please," I said. "I'm looking for Murdoch. I have to talk to him. It's important. It's about—it's about that." I nodded

116

toward the car again. "Do you know where he's working these days? Do you know where I can find him?"

"No, sorry," Julie said. "I can't help you."

But she blushed as she spoke, and didn't look at me, and I didn't believe her.

"I have to go to work now," she said. She headed for her car. I kept even with her.

"Please," I said again. "I have to talk to him."

"I'm sorry," she said. "I have to go now." She opened her car door and got in, and I had to stand back. I moved to the sidewalk and watched her pull out of her space, and then, just before she drove off, I saw her take out her cell phone. And I'm not the slightest bit psychic, but sometimes you know things, and I knew she was calling Murdoch to tell him about me.

Still, I didn't expect what happened a minute later. I didn't expect Julie's front door to open again, or for Murdoch to come out through it. He was holding his own cell phone.

"Matt," he said wearily. I stared up at him as he stood on the stoop of Julie's house.

"Hi," I said. And then, in horror, I felt that I was exactly one second from tears. And it wasn't about Nikki or Rob or the black eye that I could see Murdoch had, or the brace on his left wrist. It was, instead, about Julie, his neighbor.

Nikki had been replaced.

We had all been replaced.

25
MURDOCH'S DEMONS

I didn't cry. Instead I said, "Are you all right?"

Murdoch nodded. "Yes." He looked at me for a bit. Finally he said, "Come on in, Matt. We'll talk." He closed Julie's door, checked it to make sure it was locked, and turned to his own front door next to it. I followed him into his territory, familiar with it, but painfully aware that I didn't belong there in his house, not anymore. But the smashed truck windows, and Murdoch's black and blue eye, and the brace he was wearing on his left wrist kept me anchored in the moment. There were things that had to be said.

I sat down at Murdoch's kitchen table when he invited me to. I watched him measure coffee into the coffee-maker, fill it with water, and press the Start button. Then he turned, his back against the counter, and looked at me again. "What's up?" he said.

"I'm sorry," I said. For a bare second, I glanced at his face, his wrist. Then away.

"You didn't do anything." Murdoch didn't sound angry, just tired.

"*She* did," I said. The word came spitting out, and then I couldn't stop talking. "That was *her* last night. Did you realize that? That was her. My mother. That guy, she brought him home. She wanted him to beat you up. His name's Rob. She did it. She did it all."

Some expression moved behind Murdoch's eyes. I couldn't read it.

"Did you realize that?" I demanded again.

"No," Murdoch said finally. "I just thought he was some drunken madman." He shifted, lifting his left wrist. "The wrist is just an old work injury, by the way. It aches sometimes and I need a little support."

"What'd you do to him?" I asked. "It can't have been too bad, because he was over last night afterward—" I stopped. Then I said, "But actually, I didn't see him. I just heard him."

"I don't know what I did, exactly," Murdoch said. "I hit him a few times. I convinced him to go away. That's all I know."

"He's big," I said doubtfully. I wasn't sure I believed that Murdoch didn't know where he'd hit Rob, and how hard, and exactly what kind of damage it had done.

Murdoch shrugged. "So? Last night, he was also drunk and slow. Some big men never learn how to fight, Matt.

They think they don't need to, because of their size. He's one of those. There was really no problem."

"But—"

"Really, Matt. You never have to worry about me in a fight. Believe me." There was an ease to him as he talked about this. I remembered the convenience store, and believed him.

"Your truck, though," I said. "The glass."

"Insurance will take care of it." He sounded calm. "It's just an inconvenience."

"I don't think you've understood what I'm saying here," I said. "She did this. Don't you get it? *She* did it!"

"I understand, Matt," Murdoch said mildly.

The coffeemaker beeped. Murdoch turned to it, reaching for two mugs with his right hand. I leaped up to help, got the mugs away from him and poured the coffee. He let me. "There's milk in the fridge," he said. I got the milk out, and paused to look at a picture on the refrigerator of an elderly couple. It hadn't been there when we used to come over to Murdoch's house before.

"Is that your parents?" I asked.

"No," said Murdoch. There was an edge to his voice.

"Oh," I said. Somehow, the tension in the room had risen.

Murdoch sighed. He took in an audible breath. "Well, here's one way to look at it. Your mother was getting her rage out of her system. One black eye and some broken glass are a pretty small price to pay."

I think it was a few weeks after the Rob incident that I found out about the abusive phone messages Nikki had been leaving regularly on Murdoch's voice mail. Once I knew about that, I understood that he'd been downplaying his reaction for my benefit. Or maybe he really did believe she would stop now. But at the time, hearing Murdoch seem to shrug off what had happened to him and his truck, I was furious. It seemed to me that he didn't get it; wasn't taking it—wasn't taking Nikki—seriously enough.

"No," I said. "You don't understand. It's not out of her system. She's just getting started. She's got other plans for you."

"Have a seat," Murdoch said.

I ignored him. I gulped down a mouthful of coffee and milk and sugar. "She's just getting started," I said again.

"Well, I'm going to sit," Murdoch said. "You can join me if you like." He turned the chair away from the table so that he faced me as I paced in the small area of the kitchen. I walked back and forth, back and forth. The coffee sloshed perilously around in my mug.

"You'd better believe me about her," I said. "You have to believe me. You didn't get hurt enough last night to make her happy. She's nowhere near through. I don't even know what would make her happy."

"Me dead?"

I scowled. "That's not funny, Murdoch."

"I wasn't laughing. I was asking. What exactly should

I be afraid of here?" He still sounded only slightly interested; nowhere near as worried as I wanted him to be. As, actually, he should have been.

"She won't want you dead," I said. "That's no fun. No fun at all."

His eyes flickered then. I think it was the word *fun*. Nikki's word.

"What would be fun for her?" he asked.

I shrugged. "Seeing you hurt. Seeing you sorry. Seeing you in trouble. Seeing you worry. That would all be fun."

"Fun for your mother."

"Yes!" There had been an odd note in his voice. I blurted: "Who else do you think I'm talking about here?"

Murdoch drank some coffee. Then he said, very gently, "You're angry at me yourself, Matthew."

It took me a few seconds to grasp what he was—sort of—asking. And when I did, it was as if I were the one who'd been hit.

"You're wrong," I said at last. "I'm just trying to help."

He nodded. "Okay."

"I didn't come here because I wanted to see you hurt. It's not *fun* for me. Okay? I'm not—I'm not at all like her. Same with Callie and Emmy. It's you we—" I stopped. *It's you we love.* I didn't say it out loud, but Murdoch looked away anyway. I knew he understood.

I also knew he didn't want it. It was a burden.

"There's something else," I said, after a minute. I was forcing myself to talk.

"Take it easy," said Murdoch. "It's okay."

"No. It's actually not okay. And I hate when people say that, when they say it's okay even though it's not. It's better to tell the truth."

Silence.

"Sorry," I said.

"Don't apologize," said Murdoch. "You're right. It's not okay. I won't pretend that it is anymore." Something in his voice—just the weariness, maybe—made it possible for me to look over at him. And when I did, I realized that he was taking me seriously after all. He had put down his coffee mug and dropped his elbows onto the table. He was clasping his hands in front of him, watching them, not me, and his eyes, even the one that wasn't swollen, were nearly shut. To my disbelief, I realized that he was on the verge of tears.

Not so strong after all. I was astonished, and alarmed. I could feel the alarm like a twist in my gut.

"I should be the one apologizing," Murdoch said. "I get it. I sort of promised things to you and Callie and Emmy. I didn't mean to. I thought I was just being a friend to you kids. But—"

He looked up and so did I. Our eyes met.

"But you need a father, Matt," he said softly. "A real father. All of you do. And it wasn't okay that I stepped in there and pretended for a little while. Not when it wasn't real, and I knew it wasn't real." And now he *was* crying. He was actually crying. "I'm sorry," he said. He kept right on talking, just as if there weren't tears on his face. "I had no business doing that, and I see that I hurt you. All of you. Which I never meant to do. I never meant to hurt you."

"You didn't hurt us," I said uncomfortably. "It was—we like you."

"But I did hurt you. I led you to expect . . . " He trailed off. Shrugged. "You know, Matt."

I wanted to say no, no, no, he hadn't led us to expect anything. That I didn't know what he was talking about. But I was the one who had insisted on the truth a minute ago. After a few moments, I managed to say, "I have a father. I know you haven't met him, but he exists. He cares about us. And I did want a friend." I cleared my throat. "I still do. We—Callie and Emmy and I—we actually need a friend now. Right now. Someone who—who—" I wasn't able to articulate it at first, and then I found the right words. "Someone who will believe us about her. She's crazy, Murdoch. I could tell you—there's stuff I could tell you . . . anyway. You know. I think you know. Do you?"

Murdoch nodded. "Yeah." He met my eyes and looked into them. I saw that he did know.

But then he looked away from me and got up. "Excuse me, Matt. I'll be back in a minute or two. We'll go on talking. I don't mean to cut you off." He left the room.

I heard him blow his nose. I heard him using his cell phone, saying to someone that something had come up, he'd be there later on, and he'd call when he was on the way. I heard the water running in the bathroom sink.

I sat at his table. When he came back, I said quickly, before he could say anything himself, "Murdoch, look. There's something specific I have to tell you. About her. It's—it's hard to say it. I'm embarrassed, but you need to know. Even though I won't let it—I won't let it happen, actually. I even told Nikki that."

"What is it?" Murdoch had taken his abandoned coffee mug and dumped out its contents into the sink. I said what I had to say quickly, while his back was turned. I had rehearsed it in my mind so that I'd need as few words as possible.

"She told me she could accuse you of having molested me. If she did that, of course I'd say it wasn't true, but I thought you should know she was thinking about it. As a way to hurt you."

I looked at Murdoch when I finished. I was glad not to be able to see his face. What I *could* see was that his right hand had paused midair, just above the kitchen faucet. I counted five seconds while it hung there, suspended. Then it continued on its way, turning the faucet neatly on, holding the coffee mug under it for rinsing. Eventually, he turned the faucet off. I heard the soft clink of the coffee mug being put down in the sink.

Murdoch's expression, when he did turn, was the twin

of our mother's in one of her worst rages. I even thought I saw, in his eyes, those same demons, fighting for dominance, before he got control over them again.

I realized that I had seen his demons before. In the Cumberland Farms store.

Then, weirdly, he grinned. It was the strangest smile I've ever seen in my life. I still don't know exactly what he was thinking about, behind that smile. I just know now that it was only in part about us, and about what I had just told him. There's so much I do not know about Murdoch, even now. He keeps secrets. But still, I think that was the moment. That was it. That was the very second when he—and this is an odd word, but the right one—engaged. I think that was the exact moment when he said yes to helping us.

And you see—this is the point I have to make: He didn't commit to us because of what Nikki had done. He didn't do it because of Rob and the smashed car windows and the black eye; or because of the nasty phone calls that I didn't know about then. And it wasn't because of what had or hadn't happened between him and Nikki before, when they were together.

It was because of what I told him.

If I had kept my mouth shut, if I had not told Murdoch . . . what then?

I held my breath until he spoke.

"God help us," he finally said, mildly enough. "That's bad."

I said then what I had said to my father. "We can't be with her. We can't stay there. It's not safe."

And then Murdoch said what I needed and wanted to hear, and it wasn't, *Things usually work out okay* or *Just pretend things are normal*. "Yeah," he said simply. "You're right."

"Oh," I said. It was all I could say. "Oh."

We sat awhile in silence.

"I'll think about it all," Murdoch said. "I don't know how yet, but I'll figure something out." His voice was calm. "Just give me some time—oh, and your father's and your aunt's phone numbers. Okay?"

"Okay," I said. But to hear that he needed time and phone numbers wasn't what I had expected. Disappointment filled me.

I had expected him to *do* something.

26
PROPERTY

I managed to slip into school late without much trouble. I could forge a decent please-excuse-Matthew note from Nikki whenever I needed to. But I was unable to concentrate that day in my classes. It was as if there was urgent music playing in my head: *What will happen? What will happen now?*

What would Murdoch do? All I knew for sure was that he wasn't going to call state Social Services, because I insisted on that. "I don't think too highly of them, actually," was what Murdoch had said, to my relief. "They'll be a last resort, but only that." I told him that Aunt Bobbie and Ben were useless, but he shook his head. "I'll meet them and judge for myself," he said. And so, I let him overrule my doubt. I wondered what he would say to them. I wondered how soon he would come back to me and tell me they were useless after all. Would he insist on Social Services after that? Or would he *do* something? My stomach churned.

It didn't feel normal at home that afternoon, even though I did my best to suppress what I was thinking and feeling. Callie was preoccupied. It turned out that Nikki had been right about her. (She had gotten her first period. I didn't really want to know this, Emmy. You were the one who told me.) She was suffering from stomach cramps and was more sullen than I'd have believed possible; she spent the afternoon lying on her bed reading an Agatha Christie—although I never saw her turn a page—and I couldn't get a single civil word out of her. You, meanwhile, had turned headstrong and talkative. You were the one who was worried about Murdoch that afternoon, the one who quizzed me about whether or not I'd seen him and if he was all right. And—it turned out—you were the one I had to be most careful with.

I didn't want to tell even Callie about what Murdoch had said. Anyway, she was impossible to talk to while she was in this female mood of hers. So I hoarded the information and the hope. "Murdoch's okay, it was Rob that got hurt, like we thought," I said to you and Callie. I didn't even mention the smashed truck windows; I didn't want to make a long conversation out of it. When you kept on with your questions, I said, "Look, Em, that's all I know," and I pretended to do homework. But like Callie with her mystery novel, I didn't turn many pages of my textbook about the Civil War.

"Can we call him?" you persisted, after a few minutes. "I need to talk to him."

"No. He's going away for a few days. He already left," I lied. "He's fine," I added.

"But I want to see him," you wailed.

"Too bad," I said, under my breath. I don't think you heard me. I debated telling you again not to talk about Murdoch in front of Nikki. I knew it would have to be done. But not now, I thought. Not without Callie to help.

I stared down at my history book. April, 1862. Battle of Shiloh. Tens of thousands of men died. Thirteen thousand of them were Union soldiers; eleven thousand were Confederate. I read the same paragraph over and over but I couldn't seem to remember the numbers for more than a few seconds.

I found myself wondering again about Julie the neighbor—was she really Murdoch's new girlfriend? Or a more casual friend? I tried telling myself it didn't matter; that what mattered was Murdoch's promise to help us. And as I thought about that, I realized that I believed it: Julie wasn't important. If it wasn't Julie with Murdoch, it would just be somebody else. We were on a new road with him now, and who he dated had nothing to do with it, nothing to do with us.

I found myself thinking that it was sort of the same as

with Nikki. It had never mattered, except for Murdoch, who Nikki dated after she kicked Ben out. Men were always around, but they came and then they went. True, sometimes they were mean; sometimes we had to watch out for them. But still, fundamentally, they didn't matter, not to me, and not, I thought, to Nikki. They didn't belong to her the way we did. They weren't her property.

Property. My mind lingered on that word. Property. Yes, that was the truth: We were Nikki's property. We were—I looked down at my book about the Civil War—we were like her slaves. She owned us. The whip could come smashing down at any time, and there was nothing we could do about it except try to dodge; try to take care of each other.

Some slaves had run away. If I'd been on my own, I realized, I might have done that.

Behind me, you sneezed. "Matt," you whined. "I'm bored! Why won't you play with me?" You sidled up next to me and started trying to climb onto my lap.

I tried to ignore you as you leaned over and breathed into my face. I was filled with longing—to be on my own . . . not to need anybody at all, nobody's help . . . not to have to beg . . .

The phone rang, startling all three of us.

"Matt, you get it," Callie said to me over her shoulder, as she huddled deeper into her blankets.

"No, me," you said, racing toward the living room. "Me, me, me!"

I went, too, but you got to the phone first. "Murdoch?" you said into it the second you got it to your mouth. "Is that you, Murdoch? This is Emmy!"

There was a strident note to your voice. I knew it was probably not Murdoch. What if it were Nikki? I tried to take the phone, but you twisted away from me and folded yourself over it. "Murdoch?" you said again, loudly. Then you were silent at last, listening. Your lower lip stuck out more and more. After a few seconds, wordlessly, you uncurled and handed the phone to me. You didn't go far away, though, and you stuck your thumb in your mouth—a habit you'd stopped a few months back.

"Hello? This is Matthew," I said uncertainly.

"Oh, good. Matt, it's Aunt Bobbie. Um, listen. I'll be there in half an hour, okay? I'll come upstairs."

"What's going on?" I said. "What's happened?" Aunt Bobbie rarely called, and rarely heaved herself upstairs to our apartment. "Is something wrong?" I added.

"Well, yes, but it's going to be okay. She's going to be just fine."

"Just tell me, Aunt Bobbie," I said. "This is about Mom?"

"Um, Matt? That man Murdoch—was Emmy expecting him to call? How strange. Anyway. He appears to have, well, hurt your mom, but I promise, she's going to be absolutely fine, and he will pay. Men just can't get away with that kind of thing nowadays. Beating up women. Your mother has already talked to the police and

132

everything. And she's going to be fine, I have to stress that. Just fine. So don't worry, Matt. I'll see you kids very soon. How about I bring ice cream? Chocolate chip?"

"Okay," I said.

"I'll be right there," said Aunt Bobbie reassuringly.

"Okay. Bye." I hung up. No, I thought. I don't believe it. No. It's not possible. It didn't happen. He seemed so controlled today. He didn't seem like he—

But I thought about what Aunt Bobbie had said. Maybe it was possible. Murdoch had been angry. I thought about the Cumberland Farms store. In that moment, Emmy, I didn't know what he might have done.

I had this moment of clarity, though. My stomach clenched on me. I thought: *But if he was going to do it, why hadn't he actually* done *it?*

I turned and saw you crouched down against the wall, eyes closed tightly. What had you heard from Aunt Bobbie? What had you understood? But there was nothing I could do for you or anyone right then. I walked past you and went to sit down in the living room. I stayed there and didn't let myself think anything at all until Aunt Bobbie showed up.

27

LIAR

Aunt Bobbie came in clutching shopping bags that contained not only the promised ice cream, but three frozen pizzas. Her eyes darted around, noting where you sat rocking gently, thumb in mouth, on the floor of the kitchen. *"Does she know?"* Aunt Bobbie mouthed, as she jerked her head in your direction with what she probably thought was discretion.

I shrugged. You would have heard whatever I said on the phone. "I haven't told my sisters what you said yet."

Aunt Bobbie nodded. "Where's Callie?"

"Bedroom. She's not feeling well."

"Oh." Aunt Bobbie occupied herself with putting the ice cream into the freezer, and with taking out the pizzas and folding up the grocery bags neatly. "Oh," she said again. She clearly didn't have a clue how to proceed.

I was so tired. "Let me get Callie," I said. "And you can just tell us what you know."

Aunt Bobbie's gaze flickered toward you again, clearly thinking about trying to shield you somehow. Or maybe remembering how you had answered the phone, half an hour ago—"Murdoch?"—and wondering about that.

"All of us," I said. "Emmy, too. She's smarter than you think."

I went and got Callie. Our apartment was small; sound carried. I knew she'd have heard the phone and whatever I had said into it as clearly as you had. The only strange thing was that she hadn't come to ask questions right away. I guessed she was really feeling sick.

At least she was sitting up on her bed when I got to the bedroom, her face taut and wary and very, very pale. "Mom?" she said.

"Something happened to her. But I guess she's going to be okay. Come on. Aunt Bobbie, uh, brought pizza and ice cream."

Callie grimaced. "I'm never eating again."

In the kitchen, I got you up off the floor and into a chair. Aunt Bobbie bought herself time by turning on the oven to preheat, taking the wrappings off the pizzas, and then placing each of them on an individual sheet made from two layers of tin foil. "There," she said. "That'll work."

I couldn't stand her fiddling around anymore. "Aunt Bobbie told me," I said to my sisters tensely, "that Murdoch beat Mom up today."

"Good," you interrupted fiercely.

There was a little silence while we all looked at you. Then I cleared my throat. "Mom's going to be fine. And I guess she's talked to the police about Murdoch."

More silence.

"Where is she?" said Callie to Aunt Bobbie.

"Your mom was at the hospital for a while and then she went to the police station. She called me from there and asked me to check in on you kids." Aunt Bobbie paused. "That's really all I know."

"How's she hurt?"

"Well, I haven't seen her."

"What'd she say?" Callie persisted.

"Just that she was going to be fine. I guess she'll be home later. We'll know then."

We sat there a while longer. The oven buzzer sounded. Aunt Bobbie got up to put the pizzas in. I watched her set the timer. She didn't seem to want to sit down after that. She fussed with the top of the stove, cleaning away crumbs.

Aunt Bobbie was doing everything she could think of for us, and that pretty much meant food. But it wasn't even four o'clock yet. Way too early for dinner.

I kept looking at the clock. I had been with Murdoch until nearly noon. And when I left, he'd been on the phone with one of the guys on his crew. I'd heard him say that he needed a ride out to Newton, where their current job was located, and would this guy come pick him up?

Meanwhile, Nikki should have been in Boston, at her own job at a medical office.

A few questions occurred to me. First, when you head out to beat up a woman, would you really have one of your employees drive you there?

Also, would you march into an office building in broad daylight and beat someone up right in front of whoever was there?

"When exactly did this all happen?" I asked Aunt Bobbie.

"Well, today."

"When today? An hour ago? Two hours ago?"

"Sometime this morning, I think," Aunt Bobbie said. "Nikki called me right before three. She was at the police station then."

I frowned. "Were there witnesses? Anybody see this happen?"

"I don't know," said Aunt Bobbie. "I guess. I don't really know. I didn't think to ask anything like that. I was just concerned that she was okay."

I could feel Callie looking at me. You were looking, too.

"Why are you asking these questions?" Aunt Bobbie said. "You sound like a policeman, Matt."

I shrugged. "I just wondered."

And this is where Aunt Bobbie surprised me for the first time. "Nikki was a big liar when we were kids," she said thoughtfully. "I can't even remember how many times she got me in trouble, saying I'd done things I hadn't."

"Liar," you said intensely.

I remembered Murdoch taking Aunt Bobbie's phone number that morning. *I'll meet her and judge for myself,* he'd said.

And I decided to take a leap of faith.

I said bluntly to Aunt Bobbie, "I was with Murdoch McIlvane this morning. I cut school to go talk to him because, well, I thought she might try to hurt him in some way. I was with him, talking, until nearly noon. So, if my mother says this morning was when it happened, it couldn't have."

"Oh," said Aunt Bobbie. "Oh, my." She bit her lip. Then she sighed. "Oh, that does sound like my sister."

I stared at my aunt. She seemed entirely willing to believe me.

Slowly, then, excitement filled me. Had Nikki lied to the police about an assault? And what if I just said so to them? Provided an alibi for Murdoch? Maybe *they* would believe me, too. What would happen then? To Murdoch? To her? To us?

28

GET RID OF HER

Nikki eventually came home that night with a heavily bruised face and a fractured right forearm that had been splinted. She was smiling and pleased with herself, chatty, hungry, attacking two slices of cold pizza right away. But her good mood didn't last past the next morning, when—after consulting with my new, unexpected ally, Aunt Bobbie—I went to the police station. I had gotten the name of the right policeman, an Officer Brooks, from simply listening to Nikki. Aunt Bobbie, clearly scared but also somehow righteous, went with me.

I was scared, too, but I was also full of hope. Emmy, you see, I thought I had the means to get rid of our mother right there. It wasn't anything like I had expected, but I thought I could get her put in jail for a while. I wasn't sure for what—bearing false witness or lying or trying to frame someone; something like that. Claiming somebody had done something criminal that he hadn't actually done must be some kind of crime, I thought.

But I was wrong. The Massachusetts system of police and courts wasn't going to bother seriously with someone like Nikki. She just wasn't bad enough . . . except to me. Except to us.

It had all come to a head inside me. I knew, for the first time, fully and consciously, what I really wanted. The words beat in me like a drum.

Get rid of her. Get rid of her. Get rid of her.

This was different from what I had always thought before, and what I had told Murdoch I wanted: *Get us away from her*.

I don't really want to remember much about the next couple of weeks, so I will just state the facts. The police—particularly Officer Brooks—were offhandedly kind to me. Officer Brooks had this casual just-doing-a-job quality that you never see in the cops on TV. He was not intense and committed. Nikki wasn't a big deal to him. She was just a minor wacko; some woman who got her new boyfriend to beat her up so she could blame her old boyfriend for abuse. It wasn't anything he hadn't seen before, and he sorted her, and me, out quickly, efficiently, and with indifference.

Nikki's story was that Murdoch had assaulted her mid-morning. My story was that I'd been with him then, and so that was impossible. Murdoch's story was the same as mine; except it turned out that when he was initially questioned, he didn't say that I was with him. Trying to protect me from Nikki's anger if she found out, I figured. "He said he thought her story would fall down some other way," Officer Brooks told me.

Without too much difficulty, after questioning Nikki, the police found Rob—whose full name was Robert T. Borodetsky. The whole business from before, of Nikki asking Rob to assault Murdoch, and Murdoch fighting back, came out.

"She told me I owed it to her after that," Rob said, according to Aunt Bobbie, who went to Boston Municipal Court to hear the trial that took place before the district judge. "She said that the only way to get her ex-boyfriend was if she did it on her own. So I did hit her, yes. I just did what she asked. She told me it didn't even hurt." Rob was not a very smart man. On the other hand, we never heard a peep about him again, so maybe he was smarter than I give him credit for.

I wasn't asked to be at the trial or talk to the judge. All I had to do was sign a statement. I would have gone to the trial, but Officer Brooks told me not to, and I didn't dare disobey. Murdoch didn't go, either; just Nikki and Rob, and Aunt Bobbie went only because I begged her to.

When it was over, Rob got five days in jail, and Nikki got a lecture from the judge and some kind of probation involving anger management counseling.

Privately, I had gotten some counseling, too, from Officer Brooks. He took me aside. "Kid." Again, he was not unkind, just blunt. "What were you thinking, hanging out with your mother's ex-boyfriend? There's no reason to do that. Just let your mom know you love her. Okay?"

I didn't answer him. He was just giving me another variant on *Go back to normal*. I wondered about Murdoch's promise to figure something out. I wondered if that was still on. He hadn't called me, and he didn't for some time afterward.

I didn't call or go see him, either. At first, I was waiting for him to contact me. And then when he didn't, I couldn't be the one to call. Not this time. I suddenly was sick of the way I'd obsessed over him. He couldn't help. He didn't want to, not really. And it was impossible to help us, even if he did want to. Nobody and nothing could help, unless God struck Nikki with a thunderbolt.

My tentative new understanding, or whatever it was, with Aunt Bobbie didn't comfort me much. She was better than nothing, but she wasn't Murdoch. She wasn't the dream. I still didn't think much of her, you see.

There were two more little pieces of fallout. The first one was that Murdoch got a restraining order against Nikki. The important part of it was a no-contact clause; she was not supposed to telephone him, write to him, or send anyone else to talk to him or call him on her behalf. She was also supposed to stay physically at least one hundred yards away. Of course, this made her furious.

The second piece of fallout was that Nikki now hated me, and showed it at every opportunity. At least the fact that I was now the prime target was good news for Callie and for you. Especially for you, Emmy. I was worried about you. You had gotten a little wild, and very defiant. If not for the fact that our mother was focused on me, she would have noticed.

Apart from that, though, as far as I knew, nothing had changed, even though I had been believed, and not only by Murdoch, but by Aunt Bobbie, by the police, and by that judge.

Emmy, I remember taking you to the park. It was right after I finally understood that nothing was going to change in our lives after all. I remember pushing you on a swing. You pumped your feet furiously, fiercely. "Matt!" you yelled. "Push more!" But your swing was going too fast, too high, and I was going to grab it, to force you to slow down and be safe. And then, I didn't. Instead, I stepped out of the way. I watched you and wondered for several endless minutes if it would be best for you if the swing were to fly over the top, if you were to fall and crack your head open and die, so you didn't have to grow up with Nikki in charge.

29
ALLIES

Winter came. I was now fourteen and a half, Callie was thirteen, and you were six and a half.

Nikki had gotten weirder and weirder after the whole Rob business ended with Murdoch getting a restraining order against her. In Massachusetts, anyway, restraining orders are nearly worthless. If a person—say an ex-husband or an ex-boyfriend—really wants to hurt you, or kill you, he won't stop because of a piece of paper. People don't know what else to do, though, if they're scared, so they go to court and get the restraining order, knowing that a true wacko won't care.

Our mother, Nicole Marie Walsh, was a true wacko. I know that I was obsessed with Murdoch, too. But nothing I did could compare to our mother.

Nikki had taken some sick leave from work. She had

that fractured arm and couldn't use the computer, she said. I was at this point getting the silent treatment from her. She would stare at me every time we happened to be in the same room, and then she would point to the door to indicate that I should leave, even if I had been in the room first.

I know that doesn't sound so bad, Emmy. But maybe you remember a little about how she could be. I knew she was waiting, until her counseling sessions and probation were over with, or maybe until Aunt Bobbie wasn't around as much as she suddenly was. Nikki's contemptuous pointing was by no means going to be my only punishment for betraying her. It was just what she was starting out with.

More would come. The silence wasn't the clearest sign that Nikki was going around the bend, any more than the new, demonic look in her eyes was. The first real sign came on the Monday her splint came off, when she was supposed to go back to work, and didn't. She didn't call in sick, either. She just stayed home, sitting in the big green overstuffed chair in our living room, wrapped in her green and red silk dragon robe, not watching TV, not listening to music, not talking. Just staring into space and, very occasionally, smiling. At one point, she laughed out loud at some private thought.

"Mom?" said Callie tentatively.

"Leave me alone," said Nikki. "I'm thinking."

She thought all day. She thought again the next day.

And then she thought each day for the rest of the week. She'd get up early, as if she were going to work. She'd shower and put on her makeup and then get back in her robe. She'd fix breakfast—only for herself. And then she'd go sit in her green chair. She'd be there when we left for school. She'd still be there when we came home.

The people from her work called. They left messages.

Nikki, where are you? Please call.

Nikki, your doctor says you're fine to come in. Are you aware that you've used up all your personal days and sick days? Please call.

We need an office manager, Nikki. If you don't get in touch, we're going to have to terminate you.

She ignored the messages. I'm not even sure she listened to them all; some of them were still marked "new" when I heard them.

That week passed, and the next week, too, and then finally a letter arrived saying that she was being fired from her job, with eight weeks' severance pay. She opened the letter, scanned it, and then took out the check, folding it in half and sticking it in the pocket of her robe. She then tossed the letter onto the kitchen counter. She got dressed and left the apartment, again without saying anything. But this was the first time she'd gone out in over three weeks, except for the times she'd had to go see her anger management counselor.

The letter was left behind for Callie to read, and then

to show to me—I had been pointed firmly out of the kitchen earlier. A couple of hours later, when Aunt Bobbie got home, I went downstairs to show it to her.

"She just got this?" Aunt Bobbie said after reading it.

"Today's mail," I said. "Do you think she's depressed? Is that why she didn't call them or anything?"

"I guess," said Aunt Bobbie doubtfully. "Maybe I'll call that counselor of hers. I have the name and number written down someplace. It seems like the counselor should know about this."

"Yeah," I said.

"Eight weeks' severance. That's generous," said Aunt Bobbie.

"Yeah," I said. "She usually gets two."

Nikki had been fired twice before. She always found another job. Aunt Bobbie said that Nikki was actually good, when she wanted to be, at directing messages and organizing stuff for an office. She was very efficient, very practical, when she was focused on it, which she always was when she first got a job. So, I didn't really think it was a big deal. She'd get another job in the end, even if the severance pay meant she wouldn't begin looking for at least two months.

"Well," said Aunt Bobbie, "you guys want to come down here for dinner? I have some frozen lasagna we could warm up."

I was dying to get out of Nikki's apartment. "Sure. I'll just bring down cereal for Emmy," I said. I didn't find out until much later that, the second I closed the door behind

147

me, Aunt Bobbie picked up the phone to call Murdoch and tell him about Nikki losing her job.

They were already . . . not friends, exactly. But allies. They were talking regularly, all those weeks during which I thought Murdoch had forgotten us.

30

NOWHERE TO GO

Then one day, Nikki exploded.

When I got home from school she was her sitting on the floor of the living room renewing her toenail polish. She pointed at me with the brush from her polish, and I hastily left the room. But the tension had mounted—I sensed it—and I stayed in our room for the remainder of the afternoon, doing homework and not even talking to Callie or to you. Something was going to happen, I could feel it.

Just after seven that evening, it did. Even though I was hungry, I'd stayed in our room while Callie took you to put together some dinner. I listened to the murmuring of your voices.

I felt her before I saw her. She had come up to the bedroom like a cat and nudged open the door, which had been left an inch ajar. I didn't know how long she had been standing in the doorway, watching my back as I sat at the desk hunched over a biology book.

We looked at each other. Then she came into the room and sat down on my bed, which because of our cramped space was right next to the desk, right next to me. I swiveled, and we were knee to knee, still staring at each other.

Then she leaned right over me. Her nose was less than an inch from mine.

She said softly, almost gently, "Matthew. Do you have any idea how deeply you have hurt and betrayed me?"

I swallowed. I said, "Murdoch didn't do it, and I couldn't sit by and let him get in trouble just because you wanted it that way."

"Better to get *me* in trouble? Was that what you were thinking?" Her voice rose.

"That was your choice. You were the one who lied to the police. Not me."

"And you are the one," Nikki said, "who is disloyal. You are the one who has broken my heart." The pupils of her eyes were entirely dilated.

I felt almost as if I were outside my body, looking down on the two of us in that room. And something seized me. Maybe it was just the desire to finally speak the truth to her.

"You don't *have* a heart, Nikki," I said. My voice shook. Vaguely, I realized that it was the first time I had used her name to her face instead of saying "Mom." I kept on going. "And you have no idea what loyalty really is."

Despite my shakiness, I felt suddenly powerful. I really had hurt her. I knew it. She wasn't just saying that. I had hurt her when I had supported Murdoch to the police, and I was hurting her again now.

I was glad.

There were tears on her face. "My son!" she shrieked. "My baby!"

"Murdoch got to know you," I said. "And once he knew what you were like, he got as far away as he could. Well, that's how I feel, too. That's how my father feels. Everybody who really knows you hates you, including your children. And you say you want love? You say you want loyalty? It's almost funny. If I didn't despise you so much, Nikki, I'd laugh at you."

I was so completely focused on Nikki that when Callie spoke, I was shocked. I'd forgotten all about you girls. You could have heard it all. And now there Callie was, half in and half out of the doorway, staring at us.

And I could see you, too, Emmy, right behind Callie, peering in around her, staring at us. Looking at me, at Nikki.

My rage ebbed.

"Matt?" Callie said tentatively. "Mom? Please. Please stop fighting. Emmy's frightened."

Nikki turned away from me, to Callie and to you. "Out," she said. "Get out of here right now."

Callie grabbed you and scurried out of the doorway. Nikki stood up and stepped away from me. Her jawline was as tight as a stretched rubber band. I could still see the tracks of her tears on her cheeks, but she wasn't crying now.

"You, too," she said to me. "Out." Then she was in my face, leaning in, screaming. And crying again. "You sneaking little spy, get out! I don't care where you go. But you don't live here anymore! Do you understand? Get out! I don't want you in my home!"

But I couldn't even get up. She was leaning over me, hands on the chair back behind me. I could feel her breath on each word. The pulse in her throat was jumping.

"Out! Now! Go live with Murdoch, since you worship him so much. See if he wants you!

"I'm through providing for you! I'm through working hard to put food on the table and clothes on your back! I'm through! Do you understand me? Get out!"

But her arms imprisoned me in the chair. Her eyes fixed on mine. I thought: *In just another second, she's going to haul off and hit me.* I tensed, getting ready.

And then she did it. I sat in that chair and took the blows, right on my face. After a while, I raised my arms to protect myself.

Finally it stopped.

"Matthew, look at me," she said.

I did. I was crying. I couldn't help it.

Her right arm extended in one long straight line ending in the index finger. Pointing to the door.

"Go," she said. "And never come back. You are not

welcome in my home. You will never be welcome again. You are no longer my son."

I have no memory of my body moving, only of Nikki's outstretched arm, her pointing finger. I was moving, but I don't know where I was going. But at the same time that I kept moving, I knew I couldn't actually leave. I couldn't leave Callie. I couldn't leave you. Why hadn't I kept my mouth shut?

Except it also felt so good—so good!—to have spoken.

I met Callie's eyes as I walked through the living room. She had you in her arms, even though you were really now too big to be carried easily. You were hanging desperately on her, legs wrapped around her hips, and Callie was clutching you back fiercely. You had your face buried in her neck.

Nobody said anything. I reached the door of the apartment. I reached out for the knob.

And then, behind me, Nikki rasped, "No. Stop. You're staying right here, Matt. You can't go anywhere. You have nowhere else to go, isn't that right?"

She waited. I didn't turn back. I was trying desperately to figure out a way to go. Somewhere. Anywhere.

Then you spoke, Emmy. "Matt?"

And I turned back.

"That's right," I said. "I have nowhere else to go."

There was a long, long pause. Then Nikki said, "Make sure you understand that, Matthew. Make sure you really understand it."

31
SISTERS

This is what Aunt Bobbie said about Nikki, after it was all over:

"Your mother at thirty-five was the same lying, self-absorbed, vindictive, underhanded, treacherous, mean girl that she was at sixteen, when she used to torture me all the time." The words rolled out of her mouth so easily that I decided she must keep them in a string in her mind, saying them over to herself like a rosary. "She made me miserable as a kid, and it all came flooding back, once I realized you and Callie and Emmy were in my place. Except she had more power over you kids than she ever had over me. It wasn't right, how you had to live. And it wasn't right that I tolerated it. That I turned a blind eye. Until Murdoch."

"I called Bobbie," Murdoch confirmed. "I called her in

the middle of that court business, after she knew I hadn't done anything to your mother. And she was willing to talk."

"I knew who he was, of course," said Aunt Bobbie. "I felt so bad. Nikki could have gotten him in a lot of trouble, and he was innocent. So I agreed to meet him for dinner. He said it was confidential. I admit I was also curious about what he wanted to say to me."

"She was worried about you kids," Murdoch said. "I know you thought she hadn't noticed anything, and that she didn't care. But she didn't know what to do, so she buried her concern and didn't let herself think about it. She didn't know she could do anything, really . . . and she wasn't sure yet that she wanted to. It takes a while to decide to change the life you're used to. Also, she was still afraid of her sister at that time."

"Afraid of Nikki?" said Aunt Bobbie. "Me? No! I was careful, like you'd be careful of a snake. But it wasn't like I was fourteen anymore. I'm not so easily scared." Aunt Bobbie won't give in on this point.

It's strange. The rest of us all admit that Nikki was enough to give anyone nightmares. Even Murdoch. But Aunt Bobbie, who had known Nikki for the longest time and was afraid for the longest time, too, has wiped the fear from her mind like dirt from a window. "I wasn't afraid of her!" she insists. "Not after I grew up. First, I didn't care about her. I thought she could do whatever she pleased and it had nothing to do with me. Then later on, once I understood what was happening with you kids, I was too determined to be afraid. Once I talked with Murdoch and we realized that there had to be a way to *detach* you, safely, I focused on that. It was a challenge."

She hesitated, and then added: "Look, Matthew. Even though it was awful, it was also fun. Sometimes. Some of it. Does that make me sound terrible? That I actually had some fun figuring out how to outwit Nikki?"

"No," I said.

But I wondered, then and now, if Aunt Bobbie was glorying—even just a little—in the revenge of the ugly little sister, who in the end took everything away from the beautiful one. If so, I don't begrudge her. Not exactly.

Fun was always Nikki's word. Nikki's goal. But they were sisters. And this, Emmy, may ultimately be why, though I adore Aunt Bobbie, I will never quite trust her completely.

Please, Emmy, never tell her. I know it's wrong of me.

32

JULIE LINDEMANN AGAIN

While Aunt Bobbie and Murdoch were talking secretly, Nikki, too, was plotting. She intensified her harassment campaign against Murdoch. Initially, she stayed within the bounds of the restraining order. Maybe she meant to stay on the right side of the law—barely—and just wanted to have fun, too.

Or maybe the demons had her.

She started with phone calls. Murdoch got a lot of hang-ups from a "private number." Then she left messages that contained nothing but breathing. Sometimes so many messages came, so quickly, that Murdoch's voice mail message quota would completely fill up and people who wanted to leave an honest business message couldn't.

Then she started following Murdoch in her new car.

Our family had always managed without a car before. But Nikki used a chunk of her severance money to buy a twelve-year-old white Toyota Corolla that was missing its entire backseat and that had a blue passenger-side door that had once belonged to a different car. It ran great. And one morning, Murdoch spotted her parked one hundred yards down the street from his front door. "Pretty near exactly one hundred yards," he told me.

And then she was there again the next morning, and the next. She'd sit there and wait. She had a view of his front door. When he got into his truck, she'd follow.

"She wanted me to see her," Murdoch told me. We were walking the causeway. "She wasn't hiding. When I'd see her, she'd catch my eye and wave. I remember, one time, she nearly sideswiped me on Route 2, and then she blasted the horn like crazy.

"I called the police a few times. But I didn't behave consistently. See, Matt, I wasn't your average harassment victim. It didn't suit me to have her stop. I realized that maybe I could use it. One day, I saw her behind me in the Toyota, and I realized that we—Bobbie and I—could use her behavior."

"What do you mean?"

"I decided to goad her," Murdoch said. "I wondered what she would do if she got even angrier at me. I wondered if she would make a mistake. The police weren't going to care if she violated the restraining order in small ways. If we were going to get you kids away from her, she had to be worse than that."

I thought about that. "So you brought in Julie to provoke her," I said. "Your girlfriend."

Emmy—that was when I got my big surprise.

Murdoch said to me, "Wait. Julie Lindemann was a friend. Not my girlfriend."

I stared at him.

He wouldn't meet my eyes. "I didn't realize you thought that."

"I did. If she wasn't—then why would she . . . ?"

"It's true Julie sort of posed as my girlfriend in front of Nikki. On the sidewalk when Nikki was watching. That sort of thing. But we were just friends. She was actually in love with some guy at work she couldn't have. We were both chronic losers in the romance department. We bonded over our sad love lives." He paused. "I'll always wonder what's wrong with me that I don't ever feel attracted to the Julies of this world. The nice women."

I didn't know what to say. Finally, I managed, "Well. Yes. Julie seemed nice."

Murdoch didn't respond for a while, and I thought the conversation was over. I didn't mind; it was a lot for me to digest. But then he said: "Julie was nice. That's true. But she read too many suspense thrillers."

"Huh?" I said.

We had stopped walking to watch a fisherman casting off the dock. Without looking at me, Murdoch said, "I think that was one reason she suggested helping me. She didn't take your mother seriously enough, even after she saw my smashed truck. She didn't realize it was real. She thought we were playing some spy game."

"You didn't take Nikki seriously, either," I said. Since we were talking about Julie, I felt it had to be said. "You didn't realize what she was capable of, even though I'd warned you."

"I knew," said Murdoch tightly. "I just didn't think to protect Julie. If I had warned her, if I had just told her not to treat the whole mess like some game out of a suspense thriller, she might never have gone out to play car games with your mother that night.

"I'll burn in hell for what happened to Julie," Murdoch said.

33

THE NEW BENJAMIN WALSH

Soon after Murdoch and Aunt Bobbie began talking, Ben telephoned me. "I want to see you, Matt. I get off my hospital shift early Saturday morning. Would you meet me for breakfast at Mul's at seven?"

"All right," I said.

I got to Mul's before Ben did and was shown to a booth by a waitress who had a tattoo of dark blue lacework covering her slender arms from shoulder to wrist. I was so fascinated by her tattoo that I forgot to stop her from filling my coffee mug nearly all the way to the brim.

My father arrived and slipped into the booth across from me. I pushed the coffee mug toward him. "You like it black, right?"

"Yeah. Thanks." He downed half of it in a single gulp. He was wearing pale green hospital scrubs and a thick gray sweatshirt.

"How was your shift?" I asked.

"Not so good, actually. I'm in the critical heart unit right now, and somebody died." He finished the rest of the coffee.

"You don't get used to that?" I found myself curious.

"Well, yeah, you do. But you don't, at the same time. I'd been giving this guy a bath and stuff every day for a week. I knew him a little bit. He wasn't able to talk, but he'd kind of smile with his eyes at me and try to cooperate, try to turn himself over in bed. He wanted to do for himself."

"That's too bad," I said.

"Yeah. Well." My father stared intently at his menu. We sat in silence until the waitress came back to take our orders. I got eggs and toast; Ben got only oatmeal and juice. I waited. And eventually Ben said, "So, you're friends with Bobbie now?"

"Yes."

"How's that?"

"Fine. She's been good, actually. Good to have around."

Ben rubbed at his eyes with both hands.

"You wanted to talk to me?" I said finally.

"Yeah. Listen. That guy—Murdoch McIlvane. I had a long talk with him the other day."

I sat up straight. I had been wondering if Murdoch

was going to talk to my father as he had said he would, as he had talked with Bobbie. "You did?" I said. "What about?"

Ben was looking into the depths of his refilled coffee mug. "About what you said to me in September. When we took that walk together by Columbia Point, you said your mother was getting more, well, more unstable."

"So?" I said.

"So . . . well, what do you think now?" Suddenly, words came streaming out of him quickly, urgently. "Do you stand by what you told me? It's not that I didn't hear you then, Matt, it's that—it's that . . . I don't know. But have things gotten even worse now? What's your take on what's going on with your mother? I keep remembering what you said that time . . . about when you were in the car with her. That it wasn't safe. And now, Bobbie says she's worried, too."

I tried to sort all this out. I wasn't clear on exactly what Ben was asking. And part of me just wanted to know what he thought of Murdoch, where they had met, what had been said between them.

My heart was racing.

"Yes, I stand by what I said. She's crazier than ever. You know about her lies about Murdoch?"

Ben nodded. "I know."

The waitress brought our breakfast. I looked at my toast and scrambled eggs. I felt too excited—too something—to eat. But I accepted more coffee, not even caring when the waitress overfilled my mug again. I added three lumps of sugar, and sipped at it.

Ben put his head down and ate his oatmeal in quick small swallows, his mouth and throat moving continuously until he was done. He put down his spoon and stared unhappily at me. He said, "This is bad."

"What did Murdoch say?" I asked.

"Pretty much what you said." He hesitated. "And that we should all think about how it would feel if one of you kids really got hurt. And wasn't it better to err on the side of safety."

I said carefully, "And what do you think about that?"

My father stared at me. "What kind of a man do you think I am? What kind of father?" He pushed his empty dish of oatmeal aside and buried his face in his hands. "Jesus."

I didn't answer, and after a minute, Ben shook himself like a dog and leaned his elbows on the table. Not sure why I said it, I muttered, "I'm sorry."

He shrugged. "No. I am. Matthew, I haven't been much of a father to you. Or Callie. Don't think I don't know it. I just—I didn't know what to do."

Do you now? I wondered. I said: "And Emmy."

He winced. But he looked straight at me and said, "Or Emmy. I know. I'm going to do better. We're figuring things out right now, but I want you to know. I'm on board. I'm going to do better."

We, he'd said. *On board,* he'd said.

And he'd actually said your name, Emmy.

The waitress had returned. "You still working on that?"

I shook my head. "I'm not hungry after all. Sorry."

I watched my father watch her lacy blue arms as she stacked our dishes. "Anything else I can do for you?" she asked. "More coffee?"

"No, thanks," said Ben. She left.

Ben started talking fast again. "I'm thinking of leaving the hospital. I just had an interview with this home care nursing agency. They're going to offer me a job, and they said that if I wanted to get an advanced nursing degree, become a nurse practitioner, they'd pay for it so long as I agree to work for them once I have it. That's a really good deal. I could work weekends for them now as an RN—you know, taking care of sick people in their homes. I could go to school during the week. And then, once I'm an NP, I can earn a lot more. That would change every-thing. It would be a hard year or two while I'm going to school, but after that, I could get a bigger place to live. One with enough room for you guys. Maybe I could even buy a house."

I stared at him. What was he saying? That he'd be a rich nurse practitioner—which I knew was almost like a doctor—and we could all live with him? That he wanted to do that?

Who was this man? What drug had Murdoch given him?

"What do you think?" said Ben.

"You might try to get custody of all three of us?" I asked. I stressed the words *all three*.

Ben didn't flinch. "It could work out. I'm hoping it will. Murdoch feels we can assemble enough evidence against Nikki for me to get custody."

There was this one whole glorious minute in which I allowed myself to imagine it. I didn't feel the kind of joy that I felt when I fantasized about Murdoch being our father. But still, I felt something. Something good. The three of us—the four of us—safe. Could it work?

But I knew better.

"No," I said. "It won't work out. Because Emmy isn't your daughter, and Nikki would prove it if she had to. And Callie and I won't leave without Emmy. So, even if she let us go legally—and I guess she'd let me; she hates me now—she would never, ever give Emmy up. Even if she didn't want her, she wouldn't give her up."

Ben shrugged. "Murdoch thinks that we could force her," he said.

34

CALLIE

I tried to be extremely good after that, while I waited for something to happen. I began making the best grades of my life; I was on honor roll. I took meticulous care of you, Emmy. Through someone Aunt Bobbie knew, I even got a minimum-wage job on weekends handing out towels at the L Street gym. They let me exercise there for free, and I did, and was pleased at the results. I had muscles, suddenly, and I even saw some of the girls there noticing. Noticing me.

Maybe someday . . . maybe soon . . . what a luxury it would be, I thought, to be able to focus on flirting with a girl.

However, Callie wasn't doing too well. I had always relied on her, but somehow, right then, I could see that she was near to breaking. It was ironic. Salvation had never seemed so close.

You know how it is, with someone you know well. You don't really look at them, so you don't notice things like what they're wearing or if they have a smudge on their face. You see what you expect to see.

But I remember really seeing Callie one morning. We were coming down the stairs together, and there was this moment when she stood, her eyes blank, under the exposed fluorescent lightbulb on the second-floor landing.

Her cheekbones stood out sharply. I'd never seen dark circles under someone's eyes before, but Callie had them, and somehow, her eyes had gotten larger than I remembered. Also, she'd cut her own hair, and badly. It stood up in little hills and pressed down in little mats all over her head so that it looked darker. It wasn't hair gel giving it shape, either. Actually, her hair just looked dirty.

I blurted, "Are you okay?"

She rolled those big eyes at me in scorn.

I grabbed her hand. I pulled her downstairs and out onto the street. And there, I poured out everything Ben had said, everything I had learned about the alliance that had formed between Murdoch and Aunt Bobbie and Ben, and their secret plan to somehow force Nikki to give up custody of all of us—plus Ben's new willingness to take Emmy, and his ideas about becoming a nurse practitioner. She listened to it all without saying a word, and then she just shrugged.

"Callie?" I said. "Didn't you hear what I just told you?"

She shook her head. "No. I didn't hear a thing. Not a

word. And I don't want to hear it, Matt. I'm so tired of your fantasies and your dreams." And then she put her hands into the straps of her backpack and turned and ran as fast as she could away from me.

"Callie!" I shouted after her. "I'm telling the truth!"

But she didn't turn back. She kept running, right down the sidewalk.

35

A FAMILY CHRISTMAS

All this time, Nikki continued stalking Murdoch. She followed him in her car, watching whatever he did, and with whom. There were the calls, too—his home phone ringing repeatedly in the middle of the night. He allowed all of this to happen, keeping track in a notebook of three-a.m. calls and empty voice mail messages and of when he saw her or her car behind him. Periodically, he reported it to the police, who would usually give Nikki another warning. "I stopped ignoring her. I started getting these things on the books," Murdoch said to me later. "One violation after another, all of them small, but each one lengthening her police record. Also, I got pretty friendly with Officer Brooks.

We even went out for a beer a few times. He's a nice guy."

At one point, after Nikki had strayed twice—and provably—inside the hundred yards' distance that she was supposed to keep away from Murdoch, Officers Brooks and Coughlin picked her up and she ended up spending two nights in jail. That was in December, on the weekend before Christmas, which was on a Monday that year.

Do you remember, Emmy? For us, it was a wonderful weekend. Aunt Bobbie had gone to the hearing and came home Friday afternoon with official permission from the judge—and from Nikki herself—to care for all three of us. The doors of Aunt Bobbie's apartment, and of ours, were thrown open, and the two floors felt like one big space, one big house. The college kids who rented the first-floor apartment had all left for the holidays, and so we felt completely free in that house in a way we never had before. There was lots of running up and down the stairs, and lots of shouting up and down, too. You were playing some game that involved taking only giant steps; Callie was smiling again, even at me. Then, that evening at seven o'clock, the doorbell rang. I was the one who answered the door.

It was Ben, hauling a Christmas tree, a five-footer. "Hi, Matt." He smiled, even though behind the smile he looked a little nervous. "Bobbie told me it was okay to come over."

I was pretty stunned, seeing him. I couldn't remember

the last time I'd seen him at our house. "Yeah. Um . . . you need help with that thing?"

"No, but if you'll take my car keys, there's more stuff in the trunk to bring in. Just a few bags. I'm parked right across the street." He motioned with his chin.

I took his keys, but helped him first to bring the tree up one flight and into Aunt Bobbie's living room. As we entered, Callie said "Daddy" in enormous surprise—and then pleasure. And you, Emmy, you stared at Ben, and then clutched desperately at Aunt Bobbie's leg like a child much younger than you were. Aunt Bobbie heaved you up and held you, while you peeked once or twice at Ben. Finally, Callie broke the spell by saying pragmatically: "Where should we set up the tree?"

"Who's that?" you whispered to me, as Ben turned to survey the room. "Callie's daddy?"

Silence again. I didn't know where to look. And then Ben came forward and looked right in your face. "I'm Ben," he said. "I'm Callie and Matt's daddy, yes. And your friend."

You held out your hand like a princess. Ben took it gently and shook it.

"Hello, Ben," you said. And then you added thoughtfully: "Murdoch's my friend, too."

"And mine," said Ben gravely.

"Good," you said.

It was suddenly too much, too good—I had to leave the room. "I'll go get that other stuff," I blurted.

I ran downstairs to Ben's car, where I found boxes of ornaments, obviously newly purchased, and another bag full of wrapped presents.

I wondered where Nikki was at that exact moment. Had she already had dinner at the jail? What kind of food? What would her cell, her bed, be like? Had they made her wear a prison uniform?

And how would she get along with the other prisoners? Would she get hassled, or could she defend herself? I honestly didn't know. Just because I found her formidable didn't mean that she really was. She was slender, pretty. Not physically strong. I'd seen prisons in television shows and movies, but that wasn't the same as reality. What would it be like for her? What would she be thinking or feeling right then?

I filled my arms with Ben's presents and thought, *Right now, at this very second, our mother is in jail.* And meanwhile, her kids are running around her house, happy, while her ex-husband and her sister plan a family party.

I thought: *I hope she senses it, somehow.*

Balancing the bags in my arms, I elbowed the car's trunk shut and went back upstairs, laden down with the ornaments and with all of the gifts from Ben.

We put Christmas carols on and trimmed the tree. We put the presents under it. Among them was a big pink box labeled "Emmy," which inspired great interest from you. We received the take-out pizza that Aunt

173

Bobbie had ordered, and then ate it while lying around her living room, listening to more carols and playing a very long, very noisy game of war that Callie organized and which required the use of three intermingled decks of cards.

The card game didn't need much concentration—except that you were really into it—so we had lots of time to just talk, idly. You sat between Aunt Bobbie's legs and leaned intently over your cards, refusing help. Callie and I sat on either side of you, and Ben sprawled on the other side of the circle. This put Ben across from you. I saw you steal glances at him from time to time. I wondered if Ben was remembering his talk with me, his comment about maybe being able to take you, too, if things happened the way he and Murdoch and Aunt Bobbie thought they might. The way that this jail term of Nikki's now seemed to indicate they might. And I watched Aunt Bobbie smooth your hair from time to time.

All at once there were possibilities in our little world, and they were near enough to smell and touch.

Of course, I had felt this way before, with Murdoch. Now Murdoch wasn't there, but it felt as if he was. We would none of us have been there together without him.

That dumb, sad song "Frosty the Snowman" came on the radio, and Callie threw back her head and began to sing. You joined right in, screeching, and then so did I, and finally, laughing, so did the adults. I had not known Ben could sing, but he had a nice voice. Aunt Bobbie croaked like a frog. We all laughed at her, and she said, "I can't help it!" and sang even louder, to punish us.

This was our real family, at Christmastime.

36

CHRISTMAS EVE

The atmosphere in the house altered on the day of Christmas Eve. Nikki was due to return home, but exactly when, we weren't sure. The whole day felt oppressive with waiting.

That morning, as if preparing for a siege, Aunt Bobbie closed all the doors, separating the house back into its individual apartments. Around noon, as I paced the second-floor landing restlessly, I encountered Callie coming down the stairs in her coat, with her purse slung over her shoulder.

"Matt, can you play with Emmy for a couple of hours? Bring her down here to Aunt Bobbie's, maybe?" The relaxed Callie of the last two days was gone, as if she had never been.

"Sure," I said. "Where are you going?"

"Shopping. I was thinking of getting some decorations for the apartment. Just a little tree or mistletoe. Mom will like it if things are cheerful." Callie hesitated. "Maybe I should get a welcome home sign?"

I was silent.

Callie bit her lip. "Listen, Matt, did you get Mom anything?"

I shrugged. I had thought seriously about buying Nikki a Christmas present. I had even gone to the jewelry department at Macy's and spent ten minutes staring at dangly earrings.

"No," I said defiantly. "I got stuff for Emmy, plus for you and Aunt Bobbie, and I went out yesterday and got something for Ben, too."

"I'm sure Daddy gave you money in his Christmas card," said Callie. "Just like he did me. So give me ten bucks now. I'll pick something up for Mom and put your name on it."

"She'll stay mad at me, present or no present."

"Just give me the money, Matt."

"Callie . . . "

"Ten bucks."

"Okay, then. Listen, there were earrings over at Macy's . . . " I gave her a twenty-dollar bill, because it was all I had.

She didn't look at it. She balled the bill up in her fist and literally shoved me out of her way. "Keep an eye on Emmy."

I watched her go. I'd felt close to her again these last two days—sure of things changing. But it was clear to me right then that Callie didn't share my certainty. Buying a welcome home sign to greet Nikki on her return from jail? It was a terrible idea, wasn't it?

What did we think Nikki would be like after her time in jail? I can't answer for anyone but myself. I expected her to be the same. Maybe angrier than usual. It was only two days, and she hadn't been in some maximum security prison filled with murderers and surrounded by electrified fences. It was only the county jail, which was a nice modern brick building with pillars out front, a building that you wouldn't look at twice unless you already knew what it was.

And yet, deeper down, I also hoped for something different. That one last time, I hoped that Nikki would be—well, what are the words for someone who has undergone a transformation? Born again. Saved. Redeemed. I secretly wondered if something like that could happen to Nikki in jail. "I've seen the light! I did some bad things and I understand that now. I'm going to change. It's Christmas." And then music would play.

That night, my imagined melodrama faded away from even the back of my mind as soon as the front door opened. Then I heard the distinct stomp of Nikki's boots on the downstairs landing, and it was not the step of a woman who had decided to walk with God.

I met Aunt Bobbie's eyes. We were all in her living

room, where she had been playing Christmas carols softly on the radio for the last hour. Aunt Bobbie got up and smoothed her red T-shirt over her hips. She moved heavily to the door and out into the hall. Callie followed her, but you and I didn't move. We stayed on Aunt Bobbie's sofa and listened.

"Nikki! Welcome home," said Aunt Bobbie.

"Hi, Mom," Callie said.

"We've been waiting Christmas dinner for you," said Aunt Bobbie. There was a pause, in which I imagined Nikki, a few steps below the second floor on the staircase, looking up at her sister and her daughter, with what expression I couldn't decide. But then Aunt Bobbie spilled all her nervousness into the silence.

"Nikki, we're all set to go with dinner in my apartment. We've just been waiting for you. There's a turkey that I cooked, and it's out of the oven and resting now, and I made my cranberry chutney and my onion stuffing, and there's baked potatoes and creamed corn and, oh, guess what? Callie made a big salad with some interesting stuff in it. What was it, Callie? Wait, I remember now, honey-glazed walnuts and raisins. And I have rolls all ready to pop into the oven—we were just waiting for you, like I said—so they'll be warm when we eat. And dessert, there's dessert. I got a chocolate cake and a mince pie and some cupcakes from the bakery because I knew Emmy would like them. So, it's a real family Christmas dinner we've got planned here."

This speech did not actually come out of Aunt Bobbie's mouth all at once like that. Every sentence or so, she would stop, giving Nikki the chance to say something. When Nikki didn't, Aunt Bobbie rushed on. But having reached the description of dessert, and run out of breath, she stopped for good.

Then there was real silence. I couldn't even hear anybody moving out there. This went on for an entire minute. Emmy, I discovered that I had taken your hand in mine and was squeezing it. You squeezed back.

I mouthed to you: *"Go out there. Hug Mom."*

You shook your head. You took hold of one of the sofa pillows with your other arm and clutched it close like a teddy bear.

Finally, Nikki spoke. "Bobbie, I'm tired. Okay? Do you get that? I'm taking my kids—Callie, where's Emmy? Matthew!—and I'm going upstairs and I'm having a shower. That's my only plan for this evening: a long, hot shower and my kids nearby. You are not invited. If you really cared about me, you'd have come to pick me up tonight. You can just eat your big dinner yourself. We both know that's what you want anyway."

The clomping began again; the boots continuing upstairs. There was some kind of shuffle—Aunt Bobbie getting out of the way. And then Callie appeared in the doorway. She held out her hand to you. You clutched the pillow more tightly and shook your head again. Callie's hand stayed outstretched. You looked at me.

"I'm sorry," I said to you. It came out in a whisper. "We have to go."

I expected you to fight. But you sighed and then, moving almost as heavily as Aunt Bobbie, went to Callie, dropping the pillow on the floor.

I stayed behind for a few minutes. I inhaled the scents from Aunt Bobbie's elaborate roast turkey. Meanwhile, I could feel and hear the new activity upstairs. Voices, footsteps. The shower came on. I looked at the pillow you'd dropped on the floor. I wondered if there was any food for dinner upstairs at all, besides cereal and some canned soup.

I found Aunt Bobbie standing just outside the door on the landing, leaning against the stair railing with her arms extended stiffly to support her and her eyes closed. She must have sensed my presence, though, because she opened them and looked at me. She tried to smile.

"You're worth two of her," I said.

Then I went upstairs.

Nothing had changed after all.

37

MEN ARE IDIOTS

The rest of that winter passed. You and Callie and I lived like hostages in enemy territory. Aunt Bobbie and Ben plotted strategy with Murdoch, and kept watch. And Murdoch was literally besieged—followed, watched, and randomly attacked.

Jail had not affected Nikki's determination or her rage at Murdoch, although she did a better job of staying physically as far away as she was supposed to. But there were still nuisance phone calls and some insulting (but carefully unthreatening) letters. None of these could be proven to be from her. And there were a couple more men like Rob. I heard about that part from Aunt Bobbie.

She called me into her apartment one evening to tell me that Murdoch had gone to the emergency room the previous night. "He'll be fine," she said. "He just—well, someone bit him."

"What?"

"I know it sounds strange. But some guy—someone Nikki found—actually *bit* Murdoch on the arm." Aunt Bobbie rolled her eyes. "Don't ask me how it happened, though."

I made a disbelieving face at her, and she relented, unable to resist just a little gossip. "Well, all I know is that this guy was apparently waiting in the trash alley outside Murdoch's house. Imagine. It was freezing cold last night."

"Waiting to bite him? Like a dog? How—?"

"Matt, I really don't know any more. Can we forget I said anything? Murdoch doesn't want you to know about these sorts of things. It's better if you don't."

"Why? Why shouldn't I know what's going on? And what do you mean by *these sorts of things*? Has something like this happened before? I mean, with someone else besides that guy Rob?"

"We just don't want you worried, that's all," Aunt Bobbie said.

"I worry all the time," I pointed out. But I couldn't make her say anything else.

I was furious at being left out of the loop. And of course I had ten thousand questions that I couldn't get answers to. I tried to put together a misty picture of what had happened on this occasion: This new guy had somehow been recruited by Nikki and had waited outside Murdoch's house for him. But I wanted details. Had the guy had a weapon with him, like when Rob had brought his baseball bat? Personally, I thought it was crazy to wait for some guy without, well, something in your hands—though I supposed I myself wouldn't bring an actual gun unless I really meant business. But somehow, this guy had ended up biting Murdoch. That was so extremely weird. How did Murdoch feel about it? Was he freaked out? How could he not be?

My mind kept returning compulsively to the biter. Had he run off after the bite? Been arrested, like Rob? If not, could the police question Nikki; make her tell who he was? Was this going to lead to more jail time for Nikki? For the biter?

Who were these men Nikki found who were willing to wait outside a strange man's house to hurt him? Was everybody crazy?

I wandered back into Aunt Bobbie's kitchen, where she was reading the real estate pages in the Sunday newspaper. I sat down opposite her and waited until she turned a page.

"How does Nikki work it, exactly?" I blurted. "She meets some guy and then says, 'There's this man I'd like you to go after for me'? And they're willing to do it? Why? Are they desperate for sex or something? Are they high? Crazy? What?"

Aunt Bobbie folded her hands flat on top of the newspaper. Pink touched her cheeks.

"I'm sorry," I said. "I just wondered."

Aunt Bobbie hesitated. "I wonder, too. But I don't have an answer for you."

"It's pretty amazing, you have to admit it."

"Most men," Aunt Bobbie burst out, "are idiots about women." Fury passed briefly over her face. "I'm quoting Nikki, actually. She's always said that. It's the one thing I agreed with her about. It's that simple."

"Maybe," I said.

Even though that was a good explanation in some ways, it wasn't enough for me. I wanted to know how she did it. I wanted details. I decided to ask Ben.

I saw quite a bit of Ben that January and February. We'd taken to meeting for breakfast at least once a week, after he got off his night shift and before I went to school. He was meeting Callie often, too. At first he was reluctant to talk to me about what he called "Nikki's methods," but I kept after him. I wondered if he had once been like the men Aunt Bobbie described. One of the idiots. Had Murdoch been an idiot, too? Was he still? Was it just the male condition? Were we all doomed?

Finally, early one morning over breakfast, Ben told me.

"Suppose you meet a woman," Ben said. "At a bar, let's say. You've had two or three or four beers. She's pretty, sexy, and she seems into you. You want to impress her." He shrugged.

I waited for more, but Ben simply drank his coffee and then looked around for the waitress.

"That's it?" I said finally, incredulous. "These guys she finds just want to impress her?"

"Well, that's the main thing." Ben looked down into his now empty coffee mug. The waitress had waved at him but hadn't come back yet. "The wanting to impress."

"But how does it work, exactly? Does she just bring up that there's somebody she wants you to hurt, and that if you do it, then she'll be impressed? Would she say it just like that—straight out? To some guy she just met in a bar?" I couldn't believe it.

"Well, not so explicitly, no. But it's still clear."

"How is it clear? Does she say, *Do this for me, and then I'll*—" I hesitated. "You know. *Do something for you.*"

Ben shrugged and said nothing.

"I can't picture it," I said. "I don't understand."

"Good," said Ben.

"But I want to understand," I said.

Ben's coffee refill arrived.

"Ben," I said. "Look. You're my father. I think it's your job to tell me. This is like—like life skills."

He seemed to find this convincing.

"Okay, Matt. Suppose the pretty, sexy woman sitting at the bar next to you lets you buy her a drink or two and then she gets all sad. She tells you this real horrible story. She's being tortured by this man. He's her ex-boyfriend, or her ex-husband, whatever. She's afraid of him. He's jealous and he's mean. She tells you stuff that's really awful about this man. He beat up her kids, or maybe he hit on her little daughter. He beat her up, too. She can show you a bruise. The police are no help. She's scared all the time. She's maybe had a drink too many, and you know that. But you listen. She's so pretty, and she's, uh, cuddling up to you.

"And finally you say, 'Somebody ought to teach that man a lesson.' And she says, 'I wish somebody would. My ex is a real coward. If somebody would just stand up to him, he'd back right down, I know he would. Especially a big, strong man like you.'"

Ben looked at me straight on. "That's it, Matt. That's really all there is to it. That conversation might happen at a bar some night. It might happen later, in bed. So, now you know."

"Aunt Bobbie was right," I said. "Men *are* idiots."

Ben shrugged. "Yeah, maybe. But it can be powerful stuff when a pretty woman asks you for help."

I asked you for help, I thought suddenly. I asked and asked, and you said no. To me, to Callie, to Emmy, you said no. And what are you saying now? That in a bar, to a strange woman, you'd want to say yes if she was pretty?

"I understand," I said to my father. But I didn't. I still don't.

38

CRASH

In the predawn hour of a Saturday morning in early spring, our phone rang. I awoke immediately.

It was Aunt Bobbie.

"Matt, can you come down here?" she asked.

I did. Callie had woken up, too, and she came with me. You were still asleep, and we left you alone. Nikki, of course, was out.

Aunt Bobbie opened her apartment door to us. She had a threadbare terry cloth robe wrapped around her, and one hand was touching her throat.

I'm not entirely clear on what Aunt Bobbie said that night. I think that I have to just explain what happened—the full truth, as I finally knew it—and not what I learned first, second, and third, as information trickled in.

Aunt Bobbie had gotten a phone call from Boston Medical Center. Nikki was in the emergency room there. She had been in a car crash, but she was going to be fine.

However, the other person in the crash was not going to be fine. That other person was Julie Lindemann, Murdoch's next-door neighbor. Julie had been seriously hurt. She was going to live, but that was a miracle, because, among other injuries, her neck was broken.

It's very possible that Aunt Bobbie didn't learn about Julie right away. Probably we only heard about Nikki's car crash at first, and that someone else was hurt. I don't remember exactly when I learned what. But I must have heard more than the simple fact that "someone" was badly hurt, because if so, I'd have thought it was Murdoch. That, I would remember.

Murdoch wasn't home that night at all. He had driven out to the western part of the state with a friend who wanted renovation advice on a house. Murdoch had taken great care to make sure Nikki didn't follow him, as she often did.

So when Nikki got to his house that night, she found his truck gone and his windows dark. She had parked and waited. Watching. Drinking coffee. And then, sometime near eleven o'clock, Julie came out and got into her Beetle convertible, and Nikki decided to follow her.

There was no restraining order to keep Nikki a hundred yards away from Julie Lindemann. Nothing to keep her from having fun, terrorizing another driver on the icy March roads of Boston until that other driver panicked.

Emmy? Here's the thing. This—this horrible accident—was our big break. Yours, mine, Callie's. It was the mistake Murdoch had been hoping to goad Nikki into making. Only, in the end, it was innocent Julie who provoked Nikki, and Julie who paid. Julie is never going to walk again.

Murdoch says that what happened was this. Julie saw Nikki sitting out there in her car, watching his house, waiting for him. And she decided to draw her off, because she thought the whole situation was like something in a suspense thriller.

She didn't realize it was real. She didn't take your mother seriously.

I have never seen Julie again, Emmy. I don't want to. I'm afraid to. We owe her so much, and I keep imagining that she sits in her wheelchair in Virginia Beach—where her family is and where she lives now—and hates us for ruining her life. How could she not?

But she testified against Nikki, who went to jail again. It was only a short jail stay because, incredibly, Nikki had committed only a minor crime called "reckless endangerment." But that didn't matter. Ben and Aunt Bobbie moved into action. They sued for joint custody of the three of us—with Bobbie's presence neatly solving the potential issue of Emmy not being Ben's daughter. Nikki fought, but the judge wasn't sympathetic to her, and all in all, it was easier than I would ever have believed. All that was required from Callie and me was five minutes in front of the judge, with Ben and Aunt Bobbie standing by and looking very normal and responsible.

We had won our freedom. But it wasn't at all what I'd thought it would be. It didn't make me feel completely safe, the way I'd dreamed.

Nikki was still out there.

39
THE PRICE OF FREEDOM

That spring was a really strange time.

Nikki spent five weeks in jail waiting for her trial, and then was sentenced to an additional thirty days on the reckless endangerment charge. Even though I knew she'd be released fairly soon, that alarm was softened somewhat by the promises that Ben and Bobbie were making. Everything was changing for us, fast.

Callie was smiling like crazy those days. It was like she couldn't help herself. I caught myself looking at her one morning as she buttered some toast, and I thought: *She's actually pretty, isn't she?* It was a huge surprise.

I have to say that you weren't so happy right then, Emmy. It was a confusing time for you, I guess. I think it was mostly about the fact that you didn't really know Ben, and suddenly we were all talking about how the three of us were going to live with him. You got really clingy. You were restless and tense, unless you were being held by me or Callie or Aunt Bobbie, who you had attached to firmly in the previous few weeks. And if you were alone for even a few minutes, even if one of us was just in the next room, you would do something. Throw a tantrum, break something. Anything for attention. We started getting calls from your school. You chased down and punched two little boys and kicked the teacher. One day at school, you screamed for an entire hour without stopping and I had to leave my school to bring you home.

Every couple of days, too, you would ask again where Mom was. It was as if you couldn't remember—or wanted reassurance, maybe? Honestly, Emmy, I don't know what exactly was going on with you. I just remember hoping it would pass, once things settled down into our new life. That was what Aunt Bobbie said would happen.

I would have asked Murdoch his opinion, because he had always been so good with you. But he had gone down to Virginia Beach to be with Julie. Occasionally I'd hear that he had spoken with Bobbie or Ben. They were consulting with him as they planned our new life. And he left a message for me once, just saying hello.

But I didn't talk to him directly. His cell phone was turned off the times I tried to call, and somehow I couldn't just leave a message. I felt too guilty. What was he think-ing, feeling? Did he blame me for what had happened to Julie? Would he come back?

When I dared to think about Julie, I blamed myself. And yet, I wasn't sorry. How could I be? I carried a ter-rible secret: I was glad that it had been Julie who was hurt. Not one of us. And not Murdoch.

One night, I went to Murdoch's house. I just felt this need to have some contact with him. But as I skulked around outside looking for signs of him, it came to me how much I resembled Nikki. Or maybe it was she who resembled me, because hadn't I started all of this, two years before, by stalking Murdoch?

But still, I couldn't leave. I looked at the blankness of the front bay window of the house next door to Mur-doch's. Julie's window. I thought about how she would never come back. Her condo couldn't be entered in a wheelchair, and it sounded like she would be in one for the rest of her life.

I sat there for a while, on Julie's front stoop. I stretched my legs out in front of me and looked at them—and then grabbed them compulsively, hugging. Legs. My legs that worked. I thought about your chubby, competent little legs, Emmy, the ones you'd just used to kick your teacher.

What had I set in motion when I pursued Murdoch? It was so strange. I had gotten what I wanted: We were free and whole. But Julie wasn't.

I stayed on Julie's stoop for a long time that night. And to this day, Emmy, I think often about Julie and what my desires and my actions did to her and her life. I suppose she was the one who made the decision that night to go out and play games with Nikki. But even so, I believe my fingerprints are all over Julie's wheelchair. Mine more than Murdoch's, although, like I told you, he blames himself, too.

He visits her. Do you know that? About every six months, he goes down to Virginia Beach for a long weekend.

I wonder what they have to say to each other these days. I wonder if she wants to know how we're doing—the Walsh kids.

And sometimes I wonder if I should go and see her. To hear whatever it is she might have to say to me. And maybe, to apologize for Nikki, and for us.

40

FAMILY MEETING

While Nikki served her time, Aunt Bobbie and Ben were busy making plans for us, figuring things out for the future. It felt odd to have these two adults taking charge, when always before I had been so alone. I figured out then that I somehow couldn't relax into trusting them completely. Maybe if I hadn't missed Murdoch so much, or if I hadn't felt so guilty about Julie, I would have been happier—maybe unreservedly so, like Callie. Or maybe, somewhere in me, I knew it wasn't over.

But on the other hand, I really wanted it to work out.

As soon as the new custody arrangement was approved by the judge, we had a family meeting in Bobbie's living room. The air was full of possibility. Callie and I sat on the sofa. You cuddled with Aunt Bobbie in the armchair and then fell asleep; you had had an exhausting, tantrum-y day. Meanwhile, Ben paced the room in a sort of in-charge way.

"Our first order of business," Ben said, "is to move you guys out of here. The thing is, everything is pretty expensive these days. That's one problem. Another is timing. Bobbie and I want you kids moved out before Nikki—well, you know. Also, what I'm finding is that there just aren't a lot of apartments available. I've been trying to find a three-bedroom place, but—"

"We can manage with a two-bedroom," Callie cut in eagerly. "It's what we're used to. The three of us can share one room again. We don't mind."

I minded. I suddenly realized that this was one part of my old life I definitely wanted to leave behind. "I can sleep on the living room sofa," I said. "That would be fine with me. I'll clear away my stuff during the day. That way, the girls can have a bedroom to themselves."

Ben nodded at me. "Even two-bedrooms aren't really available in Southie right now. Not decent ones. What I was getting at is that we're going to have to move out of Southie."

"It will mean changing schools," Aunt Bobbie said. "You have to know that up front. But Emmy"—she bestowed a little kiss on your sleeping head—"is too little to have that matter. Actually, it's probably good for her to have a fresh start. And you two—well, the schools aren't so great here."

Callie chewed a little on her lower lip. She was taking in the point about the better schools.

"Where?" I asked Ben.

"I saw a three-bedroom apartment in Arlington today," Ben said. "It also has a living room, a kitchen, and a dining room. And two bathrooms. So, a bedroom for me, one for you, Matthew, and one for the girls."

"Did you say two bathrooms?" Callie said.

"Yes."

"Can we go see it?"

"Yes. Tomorrow morning. I gave them a deposit to hold it for a day."

"Okay," said Callie. "Good." She glanced over at Aunt Bobbie's computer, and I knew she'd be there shortly, looking up school test data for Arlington and comparing it to the data for Southie. She might not realize it, but she was already sold.

Huge doubt filled me, though. Southie was all I knew. Arlington—that wasn't even part of Boston; it was out in the suburbs, at the whole other end of the subway line. There would be no more walks by the ocean whenever I wanted. Also, it would be harder to visit Murdoch.

But even as I had these thoughts, I also knew we had to go. A whole new start for you, Emmy. Also: two bathrooms. Three bedrooms.

And the thing that hadn't been said: It was farther from Nikki.

Another thought occurred to me. "What about you?"

I asked Aunt Bobbie. "Are you going to stay here when Nikki comes back? Or are you going to move, too?"

Aunt Bobbie's mouth firmed into a straight, hard line. "I'm going nowhere. I own half of this house. She'll leave before I do, I promise you that."

"You're not scared? Because she'll be so angry at you." As I said the words, I knew they were true. How could the rest of us run off to Arlington and leave Aunt Bobbie alone to face Nikki?

"I've known my sister a long time," Aunt Bobbie said, which wasn't an answer.

The idea just popped out of my mouth. "What if I stayed?" I twisted my head to look at Ben. "I could live with Aunt Bobbie, in her spare room. After all, Aunt Bobbie, you have shared custody. This way, Aunt Bobbie's not alone here. We can keep an eye on each other. And then I would come out and see you guys on weekends in Arlington. I'll still help with Emmy."

Ben looked dubious, even alarmed.

"Hmm," said Aunt Bobbie. Was that relief on her face? It was.

I wasn't sure if this was the right thing for me to do, but if it would help Bobbie, I ought to do it, I thought. I wasn't sure.

Then Callie grabbed her elbows and eyed me and said neutrally, "There'd be a bedroom for everyone."

The adults had to think about it, Emmy. Callie and I both knew I was sticking her with the lion's share of taking care of you, and like I said, you weren't in an easy phase. But I promised Callie, privately, that if she found that she really needed me, I would come.

And so, in the end, though everybody was saying it was temporary, and "we'll see how it goes," and "you could move in later on, when the new school year starts in September," I stayed with Bobbie. The week before Nikki was due to come home, you, Callie, and Ben moved into a solid-looking mid-rise brick building on Massachusetts Avenue in Arlington and I moved into Aunt Bobbie's spare room.

41

MY OWN ROOM

My new room was directly underneath Nikki's room in the upstairs apartment, and was the exact same size and shape, a rectangle with two tall windows. But the feeling couldn't have been more different.

I remember vividly my first night in the room. I stayed awake on the futon just for the pleasure of being aware of where I was. Four walls around me. No one else but me there.

My room had previously been Aunt Bobbie's home office. Aunt Bobbie had promised that we would work together to clear it out in the next few days. She had said I could paint the room any color I wanted, do anything to it I wanted. I thought about that for hours, planning my space. We had already gotten rid of my old twin bed from upstairs, which I had gotten too tall for. I would keep Aunt Bobbie's futon to sleep on. I preferred it. In fact, I hoped never to squeeze into a twin bed again in my life.

Aunt Bobbie occasionally snored in the bedroom next door, and it was the most comforting sound I had ever heard. The thought drifted across my mind that I wouldn't mind, someday, if I fell in love with a girl who snored. That it would mean peace to me.

42

THE ADULTS

A few days before Nikki was to be released from jail, Aunt Bobbie and I had a long, intense discussion about how to act when she got home. Nikki had been informed by the lawyer that you and Callie had moved in with Ben, and that I was with Aunt Bobbie. According to the new custody arrangement, Nikki would have monthly visitation rights for all three of us, but her rights weren't extensive. Callie and I, for example, could refuse to see her anytime we chose. And Emmy, while you were considered too young to refuse, Nikki's visits with you were to be supervised, either by Ben or by Bobbie. She was not supposed to be alone with you, ever.

We expected Nikki to be enraged. But would she explode immediately? Would her explosion be physical, verbal, or both? What would provoke her least—seeing us, or not seeing us?

It was strange to be debating this with Aunt Bobbie, because of course it was just the kind of debate I'd had with myself, or Callie, every day of my life. I knew there was no safe, clear answer—there had never been a way to predict Nikki—but it was good to have Aunt Bobbie on my side, discussing it.

Murdoch came by in his truck late that afternoon to get me. He had just come home. We headed to Arlington, so that he could see you and Callie and Ben, and your new apartment. Even though it was a Sunday, traffic was heavy, so it took us a while to get there. At first we were quiet. There were so many things I had wanted to talk to Murdoch about, but with him actually there, they suddenly seemed not to matter.

I settled into the passenger seat of his truck and felt myself relax.

"You're all right, Matt?" he said to me eventually. His eyes were on the traffic. "Living with Bobbie? That wasn't what I thought you'd do."

"I wanted to." I modeled my voice on his: calm, even, sure. "I really didn't like the idea of Bobbie there alone. And she won't leave, you know."

"But you understand that," Murdoch said. "That house is worth hundreds of thousands of dollars, and Bobbie wants to protect her investment. She doesn't trust Nikki to take care of it. She tells me that she's wanted to sell it, but Nikki has never agreed." He paused. "It's good of you to want to protect Bobbie, Matt. I think it's really a good idea, you being there with her right now."

"You do?"

"Yeah."

I was relieved. "I was afraid you'd think I belonged with the girls. I think that, myself. Emmy's actually being a real pain these days." I paused to see if Murdoch picked up on that, but he didn't. I continued. "It won't be simple, getting Emmy started at her new school. She's supposed to go there tomorrow. She'll probably tantrum or hit somebody or something."

He was silent for a minute or two. Then he said, "But Bobbie is helping Ben, right? I think she's even going to school with Emmy tomorrow."

"Yes, that's true," I said.

"And I'm back now, too. So, that's three adults around for Emmy. And for Callie, too." He sounded very matter-of-fact. "Emmy needs time, but she'll have it. And plenty of support."

"Three adults," I said. It was amazing to think of it. Three adults to help. Not just Callie and me alone anymore.

"Yes, that's right. Look, Matt, it was a hard choice you made about where to live. Maybe it wasn't entirely clear what the right thing to do was, because there were two right things."

Murdoch had understood.

I said, "Thanks." I cleared my throat. "So—I wanted to ask. How are you?"

"Okay," Murdoch said. "Fine." He maneuvered the truck into the right-hand lane of the highway and signaled for the exit ramp.

"Yeah?" I said.

"Yeah," he repeated, and I didn't dare—or maybe just didn't want—to fish any more. It would be a long time before I would ask Murdoch directly about Julie, a long time before he told me what he really felt. What he said, instead, was, "I have a lot of work I need to catch up on."

And we talked about that for a few minutes, and then about the new bedroom set that Aunt Bobbie had bought for you, Emmy—and you still love it, I think, though I have to say that it makes me nauseous. "Wait 'til you see it," I told Murdoch. "All white with gold paint on the edges, and this pink canopy thing hanging over the bed. Pink curtains, too. And there's this rug with roses all over it."

Murdoch laughed. "Is she actually sleeping in there by herself? I thought she'd still want to be with Callie."

"I guess she's started out in her own room most nights. She loves the idea of it. But yeah, if she wakes up later on, she goes in with Callie."

"Callie okay with that?"

"So far." She didn't have a choice, I thought.

We had reached Arlington, and I directed Murdoch to

the apartment building. We took the elevator to the third floor, and the door to the apartment was hardly open before you were there, Emmy, throwing yourself at Murdoch. He caught you, and swung you into the air, then into his arms. And for the first time, I saw him smile. But all he said was, "Loosen up a little on my neck, Em, would you? I like breathing."

Do you remember? Callie was hanging back a little at first, shy, but she was grinning, too, and she grabbed Murdoch's free hand when he offered it. He hugged her to his side before letting go, and then he was shaking hands with Ben. But you stayed in his arms for quite a while, directing the tour. It comforted me to listen to you. It made me think that Murdoch was right, and you would settle down happily with a little more time to adjust.

"And this is our living room, and this is our kitchen, and that's Ben's room, and he has his own bathroom, and that's Callie's room, and that's our bathroom—we have two sinks!—and here, this is my room. Everything is new! Isn't it pretty?"

While Murdoch got the guided tour and commentary, I looked around the apartment myself, trying to see it as Murdoch would. It looked nicer now than when I had helped with the moving in and the initial unpacking. Then, it had seemed cold and almost too big, all white walls and bare windows. But now things had been put away in the bedrooms and kitchen, and Ben and Callie had hung some pictures, and curtains.

The living room actually looked cozy. Ben's old ugly sofa had been covered with a deep red slipcover and some pillows. There was a big wooden rocking chair, too, and an oval rag rug. And a whole bunch of books had been unpacked into a little bookcase. I went closer. The bottom two shelves were devoted to Emmy's books, while the two upper ones were crammed with medical textbooks. They belonged to Ben, I knew, but one of them was open on the floor next to the rocking chair. I stooped to read the battered spine. *Human Physiology: An Introduction.*

You girls were still at the back of the apartment with Murdoch, but I felt Ben come up next to me. I nodded at him and indicated the book. "Callie reading that?"

"Yes. She keeps asking me questions. It's a good thing. I'll need to brush up, myself. Listen, Matt—did I tell you? I'm accepted for that nurse-practitioner program in the fall, like we hoped. I just got the letter yesterday."

"That's great," I said. "Congratulations. I know you'll do really well."

"Thanks," Ben said. He looked pleased. "It's going to be hard, but I'm looking forward to it. It's amazing to look ahead and think about having my own patients. I'll be able to write prescriptions and everything. And, well, you know. I'd like to buy a house. In a few years, it should be possible."

"Well," I said, "this apartment is looking good, too. I'm impressed."

Ben shrugged, and then grinned a little. "We're doing okay so far. I couldn't manage without Callie, though."

"I know," I said. Guilt surged through me again, but all I said was, "You and Emmy doing okay?"

Ben's shoulders moved uneasily. "We're getting to know each other. You know. One thing that's helping— she does love her new bedroom."

"Ben?" I said.

"What?"

"Thanks."

Our eyes met. Something was said that couldn't be said aloud, not with you so nearby, Emmy. It had to do with his not being your father but stepping up to the plate anyway. And listen, Emmy, I know things didn't end up with you living with him and Callie, and I'm not sorry—Aunt Bobbie loves you very much, and she's kin. She was meant to be your mother. I believe that.

"No worries, Matt," said Ben. He put a hand on my shoulder, lightly. Then I followed him into the kitchen, where something was smelling good.

It turned out that Ben was making spaghetti with meatballs. I'd had some soup at Bobbie's just before Murdoch came to get me, but as I sniffed the air, I discovered that I was hungry again. Hungry and almost happy, for a little while.

43

HOMECOMINGS

As I think about it, I now realize that there were a lot of different homecomings for Nikki over the years. She was always disappearing for a night, or a weekend, or a few days, and we never knew what she'd be like when she came back. What we knew was that her homecoming was always the cue for a play—an elaborate production of live theater.

I was the director of our theater, arranging the stage set, telling you and Callie to take your places, prompting you to do or say this or that, whisper-feeding you lines of dialogue and bits of business. "Don't forget to hug her!" "Go get her some Advil and a glass of water, fast." "Ask her if she'll help you with your homework later, she likes that." "Stop stomping around, she'll go ballistic."

Of course, I had to act in the play as well as direct it.

And all the while I was directing, and acting, I also had to gauge the reaction of our audience of one—Nikki—and make adjustments in our play so that it would suit her mood. Her picture of who she was.

Sometimes she wanted to play devoted mom, reading and playing with her children. There were times when she wanted to lie on her bed in silence, while we tiptoed in and out bringing her coffee or Chunky Monkey ice cream or whatever it was she wanted. Sometimes, like with the Portuguese seafood paella, she would tear the kitchen apart making some elaborate meal that we'd need to choke down. And of course, there were the times she didn't come home alone, and the audience for our little play would be expanded by one . . . or even two. Once, she brought a whole party home. We didn't put on a play that night. I grabbed you guys and barricaded us in our room.

I knew every move, every motion in every possible scenario, and all the plays melted together into an endless onstage nightmare, all of them beginning with the sound of the downstairs door slamming open, and her high heels clacking on the stairs. They had all been alike—even the time she came home from jail at Christmas to find us with Aunt Bobbie—because all the previous homecomings had revolved around her. Her and her needs, as I tried to anticipate them.

This last homecoming of hers was different. This time, I was the only one there. And I didn't need to do any acting at all.

44

THIS HOMECOMING

Aunt Bobbie had meant to be present, and she would have been, if Nikki had arrived home when we thought she would, in the evening. But instead she came in the middle of the afternoon. Aunt Bobbie was still at work. The downstairs tenants were out, too. I was alone in the house, in Bobbie's apartment. Our apartment.

I had some music on, something sort of loud and pulsing, and I was trying simultaneously to focus on my homework and the music, so that I would forget about Nikki's intended arrival that night. Aunt Bobbie and I had opted for a plan to lock ourselves in and say nothing to Nikki until we had to.

Anyway, the music meant that I didn't actually hear her come home. What I heard was the screaming.

Nikki had an amazing scream—and come to think of

it, you do, too, Emmy, although yours is maybe a seven on a one-to-ten scale, and hers was a twelve. Her scream started high and keening, and then it deepened in tone and turned into a blast like a foghorn. She could breathe through her nose like a dragon and keep it up for minutes.

The scream insinuated itself between me and the music. Until I took out my earbuds, though, I didn't know what it was. I thought it was the phone.

Then I knew. She was upstairs. Early. Already. And before I even thought, I leaped to my feet and was staring up at the ceiling, my heart pounding in the old rhythms. My impulse was to go to her—to find out what was wrong, to try to make it better—and to do it just as fast as I could. I took a few steps toward the door, and the only reason I stopped was because I was suddenly hyperventilating.

She kept screaming, and ten feet below her, I bent double and tried to get air into my lungs. And as soon as I had succeeded, as soon as I had enough control over my arms and legs, I unlocked the door of Aunt Bobbie's apartment and raced upstairs.

I could not help it. What if she'd fallen and was bleeding or something?

I slammed through Nikki's open door. And as I did that, she finally stopped screaming.

She was standing in the upstairs hallway, just a few steps from the door. A few steps from me. For a long,

long moment, we just looked at each other. In the periphery of my vision, I noticed that she had brought her pile of mail up from downstairs, where we had been collecting it for her all this time. It was scattered all over the floor of the hall. She was standing on some of it in her stocking feet.

She smiled. It was the kind of smile that doesn't touch any part of the face except the mouth. "Hello, Matthew," she said. Her voice was hoarse.

I inhaled. Something stank, and it was Nikki. The mingled stench of dried and fresh sweat came off her in waves. There was also something else that I couldn't identify. She was wearing the same clothing she'd worn on the night of the accident with Julie: heavy black jeans with her trademark Celtic cross belt and a tight green sweater that was visibly dirty. Her feet were clad in sheer black socks, and as she came closer to me, swaying a little as she walked, I realized that her feet were one of the prime sources of the previously unidentified odor. I wrinkled my nose.

"They gave me back my own clothes," Nikki said, as if she could read my mind. "But they didn't bother to wash them. Are you offended, Matt?"

She stood directly in front of me and looked up at me, and I realized with a jolt that I was taller than her now. When had that happened? And her hair—it was short. It was cut in a tight, unattractive cap on her head. I could see gray in it. I studied her face. There were new grooves

214

running deeply across her forehead, matching the gray-ing hair.

She's getting old, I thought, amazed.

"What?" Nikki said mockingly. "No hug?"

I don't know what came over me. The habit of obedi-ence? I reached out, even as my throat closed up at the smell of her. I put my arms around Nikki and I hugged her, tight. One second. Two.

She was rigid in my arms. Then she pushed at me, her hands worming their way in front of my shoulders so she could shove me away harder. I let her. I stepped back.

She was grinning now. It sent a chill through me. And all at once it didn't matter that I was taller than her, that she was showing her age—or even that all-important thing, that we were escaping her. Fear of her closed in on me again. Maybe Murdoch and Ben and Bobbie were all wrong about our being safe. She was back now. Who knew what she'd do?

My old pattern of trying to pacify her was still in control of me. "We didn't think you'd be home until later," I said.

She curled her lip. "Like you care."

"Well," I said. "I have homework to do."

I turned to go.

And Nikki attacked. She threw herself at my back, hanging on me with one arm while she clawed at my face with the other. Pain ripped through my cheek. Her weight was heavy on my back. I felt one of her legs twist up as she tried to kick me in the groin with her heel.

She did all this in complete silence.

I was the one who yelled. I bucked, trying to throw her off my back, trying to get a grip on her wrists, trying to turn my face, to at least shield my eyes from her nails. For a few weird moments, though, I didn't use all my strength against her. All those muscles I'd worked so hard to develop at the gym were momentarily useless. Later on, I realized that I'd been trying not to hurt her.

Then some survival force in me took over. I reached up and grabbed her arms, and managed to duck. To my surprise, she flipped over my head and landed with a thump on her back on the carpet in front of me.

I was amazed and shocked at what I had just done. I wasn't just taller than Nikki now. I was stronger.

And yet, it didn't matter. Fear pulsed in me still.

On the carpet, Nikki began to roll over. She was clearly unhurt. I didn't wait. I jumped right over her and ran as fast as I could, down the hall, through the door, down the stairs to Aunt Bobbie's. I was almost at Aunt Bobbie's door when Nikki broke her silence.

She screamed obscenities. All of them were about me. But at least she didn't follow me down the stairs.

I entered Aunt Bobbie's at breakneck speed, whirled around, and slammed the door shut after me. An instant later, I had thrown the dead bolt home.

I stood for a minute on the other side of the door. I could feel my heart pounding in my chest. There didn't scem to be enough air to breathe. I had to put a hand on the door to keep myself upright.

She kept up the screams for ten minutes or more.

Finally, she stopped. Only then did I become aware of the throbbing pain in my face. I went to the bathroom and looked in the mirror. Three deep, bleeding gouges ran from the corner of my right eye nearly to my mouth.

45

WAR ZONE

Over the next few weeks, Nikki quickly showed her dedication to making the house totally uninhabitable.

You could count on her screaming or playing music loudly at two or three in the morning. At any time of the day or night, there might be a bout of thudding and smashing that made Aunt Bobbie moan helplessly.

There was a constant stream of late-night visitors. They were mostly men, mostly drunk or high, they always came in at least twos or threes, and they'd party above our heads until the police came. It wasn't just us calling the police. It was the college boys who rented the first floor, and the neighbors on both sides and across the street.

One soft spring evening, one of the kitchen chairs crashed out of the front bay window of Nikki's apartment. It landed in the street in pieces, narrowly missing a neighbor's Honda Civic. I had to go out and clean it up while the neighbors gathered to ask me what was going on, to lecture me, or to pity me.

Nikki didn't have her window repaired. Instead, she just had some guy cover the broken glass with wooden planks. The planks had a few four-letter words on them in phosphorescent orange spray paint, facing the street. The neighbors were not happy about this, either. Aunt Bobbie took to scurrying between the house and her car with her head bowed and her hand hovering before her face, as if that would make her unrecognizable.

The college boys moved out of the first floor on two days' notice. Without a word about the lease terms, Aunt Bobbie wrote them a check to return their security deposit. She called the Realtor about finding new tenants, but Southie is a small, tight community, and the Realtor knew what was going on. She claimed that she would only be able to rent the apartment at a huge discount. Aunt Bobbie said that was unacceptable and slammed down the phone, only to call back an hour later and agree. Not that it mattered. Nikki slipped into the downstairs apartment the moment it was empty and did some work on the walls, ceiling, and floors with her spray paints. Then, for good measure, she did the public hallway, stairs, and front door. Nobody was going to want to rent that apartment.

The door of our second-floor apartment wasn't overlooked, either. It said, in a plain white that showed up beautifully on top of the oak wood: FAT COW + DICKLESS LITTLE BOY. She had started out writing too big and had to downsize her letters to include the part about me.

In the middle of this war zone, however, I was counting my blessings.

I was grateful that I had stayed behind, so Aunt Bobbie wasn't going through this alone.

I was grateful that you and Callie were safe with Ben in Arlington—and that the lawyer had persuaded the judge, a month ago, that Nikki didn't need to know her daughters' exact address until she'd at least gone through some weeks of probation. It was incredible foresight.

I was grateful to Murdoch, who kept in touch several times a day, even though he was having his own problems with Nikki. His front door, too, had gotten the phosphorescent treatment, and in her spare time, Nikki had taken up stalking him again.

"Don't worry about it, Matt," said Murdoch, when I tried to apologize to him. "It's not your fault, and anyway, I can cope. Try to look at it this way: You and I and Bobbie are keeping her plenty busy here in Southie. The more we do that, the less time and energy she has for hunting down the girls and causing trouble for them. Because let's not forget that she could probably find them if she really tried."

"I guess that's true," I said. I mentioned it to Aunt Bobbie that night—just as Nikki led three or four people loudly up the stairs—and she nodded grimly.

"I've thought of that," she said. "It keeps me going. That and you." That made me grateful to her all over again.

I was filled with open hate for Nikki now. I day-dreamed about picking her up and sending her flying, headfirst, through the glass and boards of her own front window, to land in a pile of broken bones and bleeding flesh on the street below.

I thought, too—and not just because it was Murdoch's opinion—that this phase could not last forever. Nikki was disintegrating in front of our eyes, careening out of control. She was a half inch from landing in jail again, as soon as she did something a little more serious than disorderly conduct and vandalism of property. She might well self-destruct. It would happen soon. Soon.

46
TANTRUM

Meanwhile, at the new apartment in Arlington, things had not gone perfectly, and it was all about you, Emmy.

I remember one particular Friday in late September. It was my day to pick you up from school. I had insisted on taking my turn, even though it took me over an hour to get to Arlington from Southie by subway and bus, even though it meant I had to duck out of school early myself. I was only missing a study hall on Fridays, I argued, and it was important to me to do this.

So, I showed up at the your elementary school at two o'clock and waited just inside the front door. The final bell of the day rang, and streams and streams of little kids went past me, and finally one of them was you, with your lower lip sticking out and a mutinous set to

222

your shoulders. You took one look at me and you just exploded.

It was a classic tantrum, involving kicking and punching (at me), screaming, sobbing, and then the heaving of your entire body at full length on the ground. At first, I tried to hold you, tried to say things to calm you down, but along with the kicking and punching, you spat in my face. Finally, I stood a few feet away and just waited. People stared at us as they passed.

You were able to keep up a tantrum for a long time. I was reminded powerfully of Nikki. Maybe that made me more short-tempered than I could have been. Anyway, after a couple more minutes, I had had it with you. I lifted you by the upper arms and held you aloft while you kicked me in the legs. I didn't even feel it. "You stop this, Emmy," I said into your dirt-smeared face and open, yelling mouth. "You are a member of this family and you will start behaving like it. That means doing what you're supposed to do every day, like a little soldier. We can't cut you any slack anymore. Do you understand me, you spoiled little brat? It's time to grow up. It's time to act like Callie does, and like I do. It's time to do what you're supposed to do, when you're supposed to do it. And that means that right now, you're going home."

I'm not sure how you could hear me over the sound of your own yelling, but I knew you had. I continued to hold you suspended in midair by the upper arms, and you continued screaming and kicking for another full minute while you stared right back at me. Then you stopped, all at once.

"That's not my home!" you said. "That apartment."

"It is now," I said.

"You don't have to live there! *You* got to stay at home!"

"Tough," I said.

"Ben hates me," you said.

That was maybe where I should have had a little more sympathy, but I didn't feel it. "Well," I said, "I guess you haven't been too nice to him. What do you expect? That's what I mean about you needing to grow up, Emmy. And act like a soldier. Or do you want to go back to Nikki, huh? Is that what you want?"

Your eyes told me you hated me. "Maybe I do," you said.

I dropped you. You landed splat on the ground again, hard. You screamed.

I grabbed you again and hauled you away. "You know Ben's better than Nikki," I said grimly. You screamed all the way back to the apartment, where I dumped you on Callie and just left, fuming.

And then, of course, came the next Friday. Again my turn to pick you up from school. But I was a little late, and you weren't there.

47
MY FAULT

I think now that Nikki was stalling, in Southie, with her spray paint and her systematic trashing of the house, while she figured out how to get to you. It was always going to be you. Of the three of us, you were the one who was most her property. You were her baby.

How did Nikki find you? I don't know for sure. Maybe she called your old school and asked—in her professional, bureaucratic receptionist voice—about the transfer of records. It doesn't really matter now. All we really know is that she showed up at your new school, before I got there, and took you away.

Apparently, from what other kids at school said, you did not yell or scream or fight or throw a tantrum. You just got into Nikki's car with her.

My fault. I knew it. I knew it was because of the

harsh way I'd spoken to you last time I picked you up at school.

I should have known.

After I realized you were missing, I called Bobbie and Ben and Murdoch. And of course we called the police. Everything was done that could be done. An Amber Alert sent out with your description and photo. A warrant issued for Nikki's arrest on kidnapping charges. But the first twenty-four hours crawled by, and we heard nothing. And then it was two days. And then three, and I thought I would go mad.

I had a conversation with the South Boston cop Officer Brooks. "The longer she's gone, the less likely it is that we'll find her, isn't that true?" I demanded.

"Not at all," he said. "We'll get her. Anyway, you don't really think she'd hurt your sister, do you? She'll be okay in the meantime."

I remembered Nikki dangling you over the rocks in Gloucester. I remembered being in the rental Jeep the night she almost drove us all into oncoming traffic. I remembered the time she took you off with that man Rob. And also, frankly, I remembered the kind of tantrums you were throwing.

"Yes," I said. "I *know* she would." I outstared him.

"We'll do everything we can," he said. "We'll get her."

"Right," I said. But I didn't believe him.

I called Murdoch. I outlined again each and every thing I'd done on the day you'd been taken, all the reasons I was ten minutes late. He listened. I knew that he, like me, like Aunt Bobbie and Callie and Ben, had gotten very little sleep in the last few days. I also knew that he and Ben had been checking bars and other places Nikki went, trying to find her or someone who knew where she was. But they still didn't have a single clue.

And in my heart, I blamed them. No. I didn't blame Ben, really. My old feelings about him had resurfaced. Useless, useless. But I blamed Murdoch. He had not, after all, kept you safe.

I spent Sunday night walking the streets of Southie. I looked for Nikki, and I looked for you, the way I had once looked for Murdoch, and with the same results.

Empty, finally, I went "home."

The house now looked as if it had been occupied by the neighborhood crack dealers. Even after I passed through the FAT COW + DICKLESS LITTLE BOY door into Bobbie's apartment, I was still aware of the wreckage around us.

I went into the living room and found Aunt Bobbie dozing in front of the TV. There was an almost empty bottle of red wine on the coffee table in front of her. At my entrance, she struggled to wake. "Matthew, is that you?"

"Yeah," I said.

She gestured at the TV, which was tuned to the Home and Garden channel. A perky couple was viewing a possible new home with a Realtor. "As God is my witness," Aunt Bobbie said, "I want to be them. I've been thinking,

Matt. When this is over, when we have Emmy back safe, I want to leave this neighborhood and never, ever come back."

"I understand," I said. I eyed the bottle of wine.

"Sorry," said Aunt Bobbie, who could track well enough to follow my eyes. "You know I don't drink much, but tonight, I needed a little something."

"It's okay," I said.

"You'll come, too, right?" she continued. "When I leave this neighborhood, you'll come? I like having you around, Matt."

"Yeah," I said. "Sure." At that moment, though, it hardly mattered to me.

"Good," said Aunt Bobbie. Then she bit her lip, and tears began to roll down her cheeks.

Maybe I should have sat next to her and hugged her or something. "Go to bed," I said. That was all I could manage. I felt a sort of muted amazement when she obeyed me, clicking off the TV and stumbling into her room.

I went into my room, which had seemed so wonderful to me such a short time ago. I closed its door, and let my futon mattress practically hit me in the face as I collapsed onto it. I didn't bother to get undressed or to kick off my shoes. I simply shut my eyes and let my mind chase itself down one dark corridor after another. I knew I wouldn't sleep.

48

UNKNOWN NUMBER

I was awakened—sharply and completely, and hours later—by the insistent vibration of the cell phone in my jeans pocket.

Instantly, I rolled over and sat up. I fumbled the phone out of my pocket, nearly dropping it in my haste. The phone display said: *Unknown number.* I flipped the phone open. "Hello? Hello?"

"Hello, Matt?" A high, tremulous voice. It was you.

"Emmy!" I said. In the darkness, my eyes managed to fasten on the glowing numbers of my bedside clock. 2:56 A.M. I tried to gather myself together. To think clearly. "Emmy, where are you? Are you all right? Is Nikki there?"

For a moment I only heard breathing. Then you said, "I'm sick." You hiccupped.

"What? How are you sick?"

"I just threw up!" you wailed. "It's all over me and the floor."

"Where are you?" I said tensely.

"I don't know. It's a trailer. I'm all alone here."

"Nikki—Mom isn't with you?"

"She was but she left. I was sleeping but then I woke up and I'm sick." There was a gagging noise. "Matt? Can you come get me?"

I clutched the phone. "Yes," I said. "But I need you to tell me better where you are. Did you get there by car or bus or—Emmy, how did you and Mom get where you are?"

"In Mom's car."

"Did it take long?"

"No. I don't remember. I don't think so."

I racked my brains. "You say you're in a trailer? Is there a window? Or a door? Can you look outside and tell me what you see?"

"All right," you said. And then, oddly formal, you added: "Please hold."

I held. It seemed like an eternity ticked by. During it, I realized that it was dark outside. You wouldn't be able to see much.

Then you were back. "I looked out the window, Matt. I saw one of those big blue things."

"How could you see in the dark?" I blurted.

"There are lots of lights," you said.

I blinked. Lights. Okay. That was one clue. I said: "A big blue thing, huh? How big?"

"Oh, it's very big." Then you added, "It goes all the way up into the sky. It's even bigger than a giraffe. It's like an animal, though. Wait! It's called a crane."

And then I knew.

"Is it one of the blue cranes at the port, Emmy? The ones you can see when you're on the swings at Castle Island?"

Your voice was fainter now. "Yes. I think so."

"Are there lots of containers around, too, Em?" I said urgently. "You know—containers. They look like enormous building blocks. Are they there?"

"Yes," you said. "Containers." But now I could barely hear you.

"I'll be there as soon as I can," I said. "Wait for me."

"I'm going to be sick again," you mumbled. "Bye."

"Wait for me right there," I said. "Emmy—"

You had disconnected. It didn't matter, though. I knew where you were.

49

PORT OF BOSTON

Aunt Bobbie was snoring so loudly, it shook the house. I paused outside her bedroom for maybe three seconds, thinking about waking her, about making her drive me down to the port, where I was sure you were. But then I remembered that near empty bottle of wine.

On my way down the stairs, I called Murdoch on his cell phone. It rang and then went to voice mail. I hung up, and then called back and left a message.

I just got a call from Emmy. She's alone in a trailer in what sounds like the South Boston dockyard—she mentioned the blue cranes. She's vomiting. I'm going to go get her now. Oh, and one more thing? Thanks for answering your phone. Thanks for being there for me.

I was sorry the second I'd disconnected, and then I wasn't sorry at all. Why shouldn't Murdoch understand how bitter and angry I felt? With you missing, the least he could have done was to answer his phone. Right?

I had this moment when I longed for Callie like mad.

Then I ran. My plan was to get you back from Nikki myself. There was no point calling anybody else or expecting anybody else to help. Nobody ever helped, not when it mattered. I might even have had some vague vindictive thought that that would show them all. And that I didn't need anyone anyway.

But mostly, I don't remember thinking at all. There was no time. One car passed me, but other than that, I was alone on the streets of South Boston.

I ran up L Street and then down Broadway, on the sidewalk where they'd swapped out the regular streetlights for fake Victorian lampposts with fake gas lights. I was grateful for the light. My way was downhill, past the expensively rehabbed town houses crammed in on both sides of the wide street. Five, six, seven minutes. The ocean smell got stronger and stronger. I reached the boulevard next to the ocean, and turned left and ran along Pleasure Bay toward Sullivan's.

How many times had I taken you swimming in the safety of that big, shallow bowl of water? And how many times had Callie and I taken turns pushing you on the swings?

My feet hurt; I had the wrong shoes on for real running. My jeans were all wrong, too—I could feel my cell phone, an uncomfortable bulge in my hip pocket.

But none of that mattered. I reached Sullivan's. On a normal summer day, people would line up to get hot dogs or fries or ice cream there. The parking lot would be crowded. The contrast with its emptiness now made me feel even more alone.

I realized I didn't know exactly where the main entrance to the port was. I'd only ever seen it from the other side of the fence at Castle Island, and instinctively, that was the way I'd come. But probably the entrance was way over on the west side of Southie—blocks and blocks from here.

No matter, though. I raced to the fence and leaped up, grabbing the top. I levered myself up and over, and dropped down easily into the commercial dockyard of the Port of Boston. And just like you had said, there were a lot of lights, industrial-strength lights suspended from utility poles and strung on wires above the ground.

I paused, looking around, trying to catch my breath. A trailer, you'd said. But because of the shipping containers that crowded the dockyard, all of them approximately the size and shape of any normal trailer, I couldn't at first see any.

Blood pumping, eyes scanning, I began walking toward the center of the dockyard. I had an impulse to keep to the shadows, and obeyed it. I was trespassing, after all, and maybe there'd be security guards.

There were signs posted: Hard Hat Area and Safety First. I could see why. Many of the shipping containers

234

were stacked, three or four or five containers high, six or seven wide. While they looked secure, too big and square to topple, I couldn't help imagining them being lifted by heavy machinery. You wouldn't want to step in the way of one of the forklifts used to move a container. And what if a crane, which was used to haul the containers off the ships and place them on the ground, were to break mid-carry? The huge container would come crashing down from thirty feet in the air, or more. Suddenly my head felt very vulnerable.

I sped up, passing a row of Porta Potties. I still didn't see a trailer. Was I even going in the right direction? From the outside, the dockyard hadn't looked all that big, but now that I was inside, it seemed huge. I was afraid of walking over near the wharves, even though I might be able to get a better view from there. I felt I'd be too visible.

I looked at my watch. It had now been about forty minutes since you had called me. Were you still sick? Would you believe I was really coming? Would Nikki have come back by now? Worst thought of all—would you still be there?

And then, finally, I turned warily around the corner of a tall bank of containers and spotted two shabby-looking trailers near what looked to be the front gates of the port. One of them had a wooden set of stairs attached to it and was labeled "Office." There was a very bright light on a post just beside the stairs to the office.

Somehow, I knew that was where you were. I took a deep breath and walked, rapidly, out of the shadows of my container bank. I was up the wooden stairs in a flash, grasping the knob of the office. The door was locked.

"Emmy?" I yelled instinctively. My voice was way too loud, and it scared me. I rapped at the door instead. "It's Matthew," I called, more moderately. "Can you let me in? The door's locked." I looked over my shoulder. I prayed no one was around to hear me.

I prayed Nikki wasn't around, that she hadn't yet come back. Although, then again—what if you had passed out in there? Or worse? My fist clenched on the doorknob.

The knob moved under my hand. I heard the tiny scrabble of a lock being drawn back. And then the door moved inward, and I pushed it the rest of the way, gently.

There you were, staring big-eyed, teary, at me. You were still in your school clothes, from Friday. Also, you hadn't lied about being sick, Emmy. You were covered in vomit.

And you stank of alcohol.

50
THE O.K. CORRAL

I wish I could say I grabbed you up in my arms anyway, but I didn't. "Ew," I said. Then I noticed that you were holding on to the trailer door for dear life.

"Matt!" you wailed.

At that point, I had to reach out and catch you, because you started to fall. I heaved you up over my shoulder in a fireman's carry and tried not to breathe through my nose. I spared a glance inside the trailer; I saw a desk, cluttered with papers, a wall full of bookcases with binders on them. No Nikki, though, and that was the important thing.

I said, under my breath, "Em, what have you been *doing*? You reek."

You murmured, "She made me." Then you shifted on my shoulder, and nearly toppled off it. I hugged you hard, just for a second.

I said, "Stay as still as possible, can you? You're heavy." I started down the stairs, trying to keep you balanced. It wasn't easy, and I was grateful for my workouts at the gym. Then I hesitated. Could I actually carry you all the way back across the dockyard, the way I'd come, and somehow get you over the fence by Sullivan's? I doubted it.

Maybe we could just leave through the main gate? It was nearer. I could see that it was closed, but that didn't mean it was locked. Or we could just jump and scramble over the gate, the way I'd gotten over the fence? I would need you to cooperate to do that. "Stay *still*, Emmy," I said sharply again. Before I was aware of making a decision, I started trudging unevenly toward the gate. It was only about twenty yards ahead. I'd figure it out when we got there.

I could feel the weight of my cell phone in my pocket—maybe I could call a cab to pick us up? But I didn't have any money on me. Call Aunt Bobbie, and hope that she woke up when the phone rang? Or maybe I could just call 911? I thought about that. Yes, I would call 911, as soon as I got outside the dockyard and found someplace to put you down. It was best, too, because you had gone completely limp and I knew you had passed out.

I staggered toward the gate. I was feeling your slow breath, in and out, in and out, against my back, when I heard a mechanical rumbling. I looked up to see the double gates to the dockyard swinging open. A large Ford truck nosed in, and its headlights caught you and me squarely in their glare. Its brakes squealed as it came to a halt on the concrete road a few yards in front of us.

The passenger door of the truck swung open, and our mother jumped out. I could see her unmistakably silhouetted behind the lights, and I knew that she would see us clearly, too. She stood next to the truck for a second, and then she laughed.

"Matthew!" she called. "Fancy meeting you here!" She slammed her door shut and started walking toward us.

I don't know exactly why I did what I did. Maybe it was just that running was obviously useless. So I kept a tight grip on you and walked grimly forward to meet her, like it was the gunfight at the O.K. Corral. And me packing a cell phone in one pocket and a seven-year-old sister on one shoulder.

Meanwhile, the driver of the truck had gotten out, too, and stood uncertainly beside his truck with his door still open. "Nikki?" he said. "Nobody's supposed to come in the yard. Nobody's supposed to know I ever let you in. I told you that. It's my job on the line here."

"No worries. That's just my other kid," my mother said. We were within a couple yards of each other now. We stopped, facing each other. For a long, long minute there was silence.

I said, "You got Emmy drunk."

"It was the only way to shut her up. It wasn't hard. She likes sangria best, and it turns out she'll only drink beer if I make her, but she really had a party with the bourbon tonight, once I got her started. It was pretty impressive."

I had this moment of dizziness. The world went white for a second or two. And then, when I recovered, I was different. I can't explain it any better than that. I was different. I have stayed different from that moment to this one.

It wasn't that I was no longer afraid of Nikki. It was that I didn't care that I was afraid. Fear was not going to rule me anymore. Not with Nikki. Not with anyone.

No more.

Nikki was saying sweetly, "And I needed her to sleep so that I could spend some quality time with Bob here." She jerked her chin in the direction of the truck driver. "I needed to thank him for giving us shelter. I mean, it's his job at risk." Her voice dripped sarcasm.

"It really is!" said Bob defensively. "I told you—"

I cut him off, though my eyes didn't leave my mother's face. My voice came out strong. Loud. "Then you'd better get out of here, Bob, before I get a good look at you and your license plate. Because there's a warrant out for Nikki's arrest on kidnapping charges. If you're involved with that, you'll lose your job for sure. To say the least."

"Nikki," Bob began.

I didn't let him get any further. "So far, Bob," I said, "I haven't actually seen you at all. I couldn't describe you. I don't know your name. And I don't have any reason to want you to lose your job. Yet. That means you have thirty seconds to get out of here."

I still didn't look at Bob. I didn't need to, Emmy. You see, I knew him. I knew a hundred men like him, and I knew what he'd do. I knew what his fear would make him do.

And he did it. He got back into his truck. The door slammed, and the wheels squealed as he put it into reverse. He got the hell out of Dodge, leaving you and me alone with our mother.

She was still smiling.

"Where's Murdoch?" she said.

I blinked.

"Isn't he here?" Nikki said. "Didn't you call him before coming on your big rescue mission, Matthew? You're so predictable. Don't tell me you're going to surprise me now."

"He's not here," I said steadily. "I'm here. I don't need Murdoch or anyone to take Emmy away. Or to tell you that you won't be allowed to see her ever again. I'll make sure of that. Me. Alone, if necessary."

I could do anything that I had to do now. I knew it. I could even—I saw it suddenly—I could kill Nikki. I could. It would be easy. I would feel no remorse. She deserved death.

Right here. Right now. Put you down, Emmy. Then knock Nikki to the ground and kick her head and chest until she died.

Easy. It would be easy.

She had kidnapped you. She had gotten you drunk. I could even claim she had threatened us. I would get away with it. And so what if I didn't? Who cared? You and Callie had Ben and Bobbie and Murdoch to take care of you. You wouldn't need me.

And Nikki would be dead.

Nikki would be dead.

My mother would be dead.

It took only a few seconds for these thoughts to fill me. To empower me.

"Aren't you the big man now?" Nikki was saying.

Emmy, I leaned over. I put you down. And then I was in front of Nikki, lifting my hands to her, grabbing her, throwing her to the ground.

51
LIKE ME

I would have done it, Emmy. I had drawn back my foot to kick Nikki in the head with the full force of all of the rage and hate inside me, when a truck came roaring up to the gate again. But this time it was not Bob. This time it was a truck I recognized.

I took two steps back, away from my mother.

Nikki immediately levered herself up onto her elbows. She gave a little hiss. I thought I heard her mutter, "I knew it." She got to her feet.

Murdoch pulled up. He got out of his truck and his eyes found mine. "Sorry," he said. "I fell asleep."

I didn't know if he'd seen me looming over Nikki. I didn't know if he realized what I had been about to do. In that moment, I hated him for coming. For stopping me.

He was in front of me. We formed a little circle: Murdoch, Nikki, and me, with you on the ground. Then Murdoch knelt and scooped you up. His nostrils flared at your smell. "Whew."

You were unconscious, but I watched you turn in your sleep and nestle comfortably, trustingly, into Murdoch's arms.

What if it had been two minutes later? What if Murdoch had come to find me kicking Nikki to death? What if it had been *five* minutes later, and Nikki was already dead?

Murdoch's back was to Nikki. He had not looked directly at her. She said his name. He still didn't look. She said it again, more sharply. Still, she was ignored.

"Come on, Matt," he said to me. "Let's go."

"Murdoch!" Nikki repeated. She was shouting now. "Look at me! You look at me!" She was entirely focused on him. It seemed to me that she, too, didn't understand what I had almost done.

Murdoch didn't answer. Carrying you, he began walking away.

I couldn't follow. Not yet. I watched Nikki. How could she not have realized that her son had been about to kick her head in?

But she wasn't even aware of me. She was working her face oddly, staring after Murdoch. "Don't you walk away from me!" she shouted at his back. "You have to look at me! You have to see what you've done to me! All of this is your fault! Yours! My life is a mess now, and it's all because of you."

Murdoch stopped walking and turned, but it was only to quirk an eyebrow back at me. "Matt?"

"Murdoch!" Nikki shouted again. "Just answer one question. That's all I want. This one question answered."

I found myself at Murdoch's side. I got into the truck's passenger seat and Murdoch handed you to me. I settled you into my lap just as Nikki came up next to Murdoch and grabbed at his arm, tugging, pulling. He pushed her away and closed the door between her and us. "Lock it, Matthew," he said, and, numbly, I did.

I watched as our mother came in close to Murdoch again and tried to twine her arms around his neck. His face was impassive, but he grabbed her forearms and tried to move her away from him.

She leaned in and screamed right into his face: "Why'd you take my kids from me, Murdoch? Why? Why? Why?"

Murdoch's hands tightened around Nikki's forearms. He yanked her away. She staggered back a few steps, glaring.

He had already turned away from her. But I saw his face, and the way he stood in his body in that moment, and sudden knowledge about him came through to me. It was as if he was a piece of code that had been encrypted until this moment, but now I could read him clearly for the very first time.

And I knew he had been like me. That he had once been a child just like me.

Then Murdoch was standing in front of Nikki.

"If I were you, Nikki, I'd leave this state and never come back. This time you won't get out of jail quickly. This time it'll be years."

And then he was back, climbing into the truck beside you and me, closing and locking the door. And not a moment too soon, because Nikki ran to us again. She held on to the handle of Murdoch's door, trying in vain to open it, pounding on the window with her other hand. Her face was as contorted as I'd ever seen it. She had eyes only for Murdoch. It was as if you and I were not there.

"You'll be sorry!" she screamed. "You'll be sorry you did this to me."

Murdoch shrugged. He started the car and put it in reverse. And at the last possible second—I hardly believed it—Nikki let go and stepped away. And we drove off.

I didn't look back, but I felt her eyes on us all the way out the gate.

52

MY PROMISE

Two years ago now, Emmy. We have not seen her since.

So. Is that all? Is that it? I don't know. Maybe.

Maybe not.

Yesterday, I turned eighteen. I have plans for my future, and for the first time since you were born, they do not include you. This fall, I am leaving you and Aunt Bobbie and the home we've made together in Scituate these last years. I am going to college more than halfway across the country.

I am leaving Callie behind, too, of course. In some ways, this feels less important than leaving you, because Callie has made her home with Ben these past years. But in others, it's huge, because she is still Callie, still my partner. We spent all those years knowing, at a glance, what the other was thinking or feeling. That hasn't changed.

At first I hoped that Callie would follow me to Austin, to do her premed major there. But she says probably not. "I'll think about it. But, well . . ."

I understand what she doesn't dare say, not yet, anyway. Callie is having those big dreams again. Ben told me that her chemistry and biology teachers think she should apply to this special program that would get her into medical school after only three years of undergraduate work. If she wants.

Which she does.

Once, about a year ago, she said to me, "We were lucky, Matthew. So lucky that I sometimes lie awake at night thinking about it. And thinking about other kids, too. All the other kids out there. Somewhere."

"I know," I said. We didn't need to say more. We never did.

Callie's teachers, no matter how brilliant they think she is, never will know why she is going to be such a good doctor, such a rare doctor. But I know, and you do, too, Emmy. Callie has taken something from our family that I can't even put into words. Something I never imagined, back when my whole world was about taking care of her. About making sure she survived.

I am proud of Callie, Emmy. So proud—if a little sad— that she doesn't need me anymore.

But you. By leaving you, I am saying that you don't need me anymore, either. That on a day-to-day basis, Aunt Bobbie is enough—with Murdoch and Ben and Callie nearby, of course. That there will be no other emergency, or crisis, or peril that requires me to save you.

The thing is, despite the calm of these last two years, I don't believe it. I wonder if it would have been better if Murdoch had not come that night. He came too late to keep me from that moment of transformation when I understood I could and would kill Nikki. And he came before I could ensure your safety forever by doing what I would have done.

So now, I must behave like a normal eighteen-year-old, as if all I need to think about is myself and what I want. It's attractive. Sometimes when I'm alone, I open my letter from the University of Texas, Austin, and I read about my scholarship, and about how much they hope I will accept it, and how promising a young man they think I am. I know they say similar things to everybody. I read it anyway. I eat it up.

I want to go to Austin, and I will. But I do it knowing that our mother will turn up again one day. Next month, next year, five years from now, or when you are grown up. She will come. For you.

Murdoch says no, she won't. But I know her better than he does.

And even if he turns out to be right, even if she doesn't return, I also know that our mother is not the only peril in the world. Not the only person who will hurt those she says she loves, or put them carelessly in the way of danger.

So, my little sister. This is what I want to tell you. Even as I move into adulthood and make choices that take me physically far from you—and even as, in time, you do the same in your own life—I will stay alert. My cell phone will always be on, and I will be only a phone call (or an email, or an instant message) away. I don't just mean while I am in college, Emmy. I mean forever. And I will do what has to be done. I know now that I can.

This, I think, is why I've been so driven to write the whole story for you. Not really so that you'll remember our mother, and not be fooled by her when she shows up. In my heart, I don't think you have forgotten her, or would be fooled by her. But I write so that you'll remember *me*. And so that you will have this in writing, and understand exactly why I say it to you:

As long as I live, when you need help, you will never need to beg anyone to notice. I won't just hang around thinking I ought to do something to help.

I will act.

53

P. S.

I put away this letter—and I guess it's still a letter, even though it's very long—a few months ago. I thought I'd let it sit awhile. Then I'd go over it and see if there was anything I wanted to change.

But now I am adding to it, finishing it, without having reread what I wrote before. I will never reread it. I know that now. This letter, this story, done or not, over or not, is done and over. It is what it is. With this last entry, I close the book.

But before I do, I have just a little more to say. One new discovery that I'm still puzzling over, trying to figure out what it means. And something else, too, smaller, that I concealed from you and that has been eating at me.

The smaller, easier thing first. The little lie that's been eating at me.

Emmy, I told you that we had not seen Nikki since the night you and I left her behind us at the port. Strictly speaking, that's true. But it implies that we haven't heard from her, either, and that is a lie. There are letters, regular letters, handwritten and sent through the U.S. mail, forwarded from our old address. There's at least one a month, and occasionally there will be a rush of them, one or even two a day for seven, eight, nine days in a row. I get them, and Callie gets them, and some are addressed to you, though Aunt Bobbie and I make sure you never see them. Ben, Aunt Bobbie, and Murdoch get them, too.

Some of the letters are ordinary, crazy in their ordinariness, full of motherly questions about school and advice to dress warmly in the winter and to eat vegetables. But some of the letters, most of them, are rants. Certain themes return again and again.

I love you.

I miss you.

I hate you.

It's Murdoch's fault.

It's Matthew's fault. (By the way, she never blames Callie or you, or Ben or Bobbie.)

I'm going to kill you.

I'm going to kill myself.

You'll be sorry.

None of the letters contain information about Nikki and her life, though they are usually postmarked from some tourist city, like Las Vegas, Orlando, or Atlantic City, and written on hotel stationery: Comfort Inn, Holiday Inn Express, the occasional Hilton or Marriott. We can only guess where she lives, how she lives.

At first, I found the letters enraging, and also terrifying. I will not pretend that I am not still afraid of her. A letter would arrive, and I'd feel as if Nikki herself were there. I could almost see her hands in motion. Her nails. Panic would push at me from inside, and I'd spend the next few days with an accelerated heart rate, looking over my shoulder. Where did she live, could she be tracked down, how could we—how could you—be kept safe? Should I get a gun? Thoughts like these would claw frantically and repetitively at my mind.

And then . . . I don't know. A year passed, and then two. And lately, well, it's not such a big deal anymore. A letter comes, and my throat closes up only for an instant, and honestly, Em, I'm almost bored. I don't open them anymore. I look at the postmark and I put it away to give to Murdoch.

Is she still dangerous to us? Maybe. Anybody can be dangerous. But once she was all-powerful in our lives. She was the queen bee and we served her. Now she's dangerous like a mosquito. A mosquito might bite you. It might carry malaria. But most of the time, a mosquito just whines and buzzes. And even if it bites you, even if it draws blood, well, so what?

Let her write her letters. Let her live her life, wherever she is, whoever she's with, whatever she's doing. I can almost see her on a bar stool somewhere, trying to pick up the man on the next stool. She's older now, she's not finding it as easy as she used to.

You know what? I almost have it in me to feel sorry for her. Almost. And sometimes now, I think maybe it was good that Murdoch showed up when he did that night. Maybe it was good that I didn't kill her.

The other day, I realized this, Emmy. And that was what made me think that there was no need, really, to conceal the letters from you. You, too, should understand that Nicole Marie O'Grady Walsh is only a mosquito in our lives.

Murdoch volunteered to keep the letters, to keep the originals safe and give copies to the police just in case, some unlikely day, she comes back. He was never alarmed by the letters the way I was, even though, as I said, he got them too. I have a suspicion, in fact, that he got more of them than any of the rest of us.

That brings me to the other thing I wanted to tell you. For me, this story ends where it began: with Murdoch. I'm thinking that if I write it all out here, the thing that I just found out about him, I may grasp something I can feel myself straining for. Some bit of understanding that's been out of my reach.

I had dinner with Murdoch the other night, the day I sent in my official acceptance to UT. We went to this place way up in Essex where you could eat mounds of fried clams and onion rings. We sat at a picnic table out-side near the water. I wouldn't be seeing much of the ocean in Austin, Texas, Murdoch said. He was proud of me, he said.

"And don't worry," he said. We both knew what he was talking about.

"I won't," I answered. "Not too much." I told him my mosquito theory. "I only just understood this," I said.

"It's good," said Murdoch. "A mosquito. Yes."

We ate the rest of our clams in silence. You could hear the surf washing up on the sand. The sun began to melt into sunset pinks and blues, and these little white lights that were strung all over the clam shack's outdoor dining area came on.

"Do you remember the day we met?" I asked diffidently. "I don't mean your first real date with Nikki, when she brought you home for dinner and introduced us. But did you ever realize that we really met, sort of, almost a year before that? It was a Saturday night in August, at the Cumberland Farms store."

Murdoch frowned. "The Cumberland Farms?"

"Yes." I described the scene to him meticulously. I didn't look at him until I was done.

He said simply, "Yes. I remember that night. So, that was you and Callie? You were those kids?"

"Yeah," I said. I took a deep breath, and then I told him how I'd looked for him after that. Looked, and looked, and looked. "I was only thirteen," I said. "I thought—I don't know what I thought. But I was impressed by you. By what you did."

A pause. Then: "I ate too many clams just now," said Murdoch. "Let's walk some."

We walked slowly along the beach. And I know Murdoch, so I kept quiet, and eventually he said, "Matt?"

"Yeah?"

"I'm sorry. You were looking for some hero, weren't you? Batman, Spider-Man, something like that. A savior. You thought you found one in the Cumberland Farms. But I wasn't it."

It was true, I thought. That was what I had wanted, and I had not gotten it. But I had been a child. Now I wasn't. It had been too much to expect. I had understood this for a while now.

"You helped us," I said. "I was too close to see what was happening at first, but you got Ben and Bobbie to pay attention. You organized them, you encouraged them. And it worked. We're all okay now. We're okay, we're free. And she's a mosquito."

"I almost didn't help," Murdoch said quietly. "I almost ducked out. I wanted to. I wanted to run out on you. It just seemed—too much. When you came to me. When I understood how much you needed help." He paused. Then he said carefully, "I couldn't see my way clear at first. At first, the only thing I could think of to do was something I shouldn't do. It took me a long time to figure something else out. And I knew you were waiting, hoping. I knew you were disappointed in me. I knew you were depending on me."

"What you did was enough," I said. "We didn't need a superhero. Just an adult who acted to help us when I asked."

Those words sounded so sane, so reasonable, out there in the warm safe evening ocean air. I sounded so sane, so reasonable.

But I swear to you, Em, as I said those words, I had a flash of understanding. Murdoch had just said that the only thing he could think of to *do* was something he *shouldn't* do.

And that slotted in with my realization in the dock-yard. *He's just like me.*

"Let's head back to the truck," I said.

"Are you okay? You look funny."

"Yeah. I ate a bad clam or something."

We went in silence. I could feel Murdoch's concern, but I didn't look at him. I just focused on my feet. We got into the truck.

"I'm going to get you home," Murdoch said.

"Wait," I said. "I need to tell you something."

"Matt, what is it? You're sweating. You really are sick."

I said, "I'm not sick. Well, I am, but it's not physical. Listen. I have to tell you something.

"I wasn't looking for a superhero, Murdoch. I mean, we can call it that if we want, but the truth is, I was looking for somebody who would kill her. I thought maybe you would do it, if you knew her—if you knew and liked us. Because of the way you stepped in for that boy. Suddenly I understand now that that was what I thought. That was what I hoped for."

It was full dark now, outside of the truck in the parking lot. I waited for Murdoch to speak. When he didn't, I said, "I didn't even let myself know that was what I was thinking. But I realize it now."

There was enough light so that I could see how Murdoch's hands were gripping the steering wheel.

I swallowed. I added, "And I know why I thought that, too. I recognized something in you. You're like me, aren't you, Murdoch? Like us? You had a mother like ours, didn't you?" I thought of how I had always tried to get him to talk about his childhood, his parents. And how he'd always refused.

He was silent.

"I'm sorry," I said. "I know it's not my business, but—"

"Not a mother," said Murdoch steadily. "A father."

"Oh," I said.

It was so long before he spoke again that I thought he wasn't going to. But then he said, "You're right, Matthew. I am like you.

"You, twenty-some-odd years later. Someday—not tonight, I think we've had enough for one night—I'll tell you about my father.

"I haven't killed anyone since I went after my father at

thirteen. I won't kill anyone again, even when I believe they deserve it. But still . . . yes, you found someone who could have killed your mother. I just—I wouldn't. I promised myself. I'm sorry."

"Don't be sorry," I said. I told Murdoch, then, about the five minutes.

We sat in silence.

Then Murdoch said, "I'm glad I came when I did. In the dockyard."

"I don't know," I said. "I'm still not sure."

"Trust me," Murdoch said. "Trust me on this, son."

So. Emmy. Little sister. You're never going to read this, are you? I'm never going to give it to you. I didn't write it for you. I wrote it for me.

I wrote it to work my way through the story of what formed me. I wrote it to examine the past and figure out who Murdoch was, so that I could figure out who I was. I wrote it to understand who I am, and how I ought to act in the world.

I think I have made a beginning.

ACKNOWLEDGMENTS

With thanks for help in time of need, with this book and in life, to Franny Billingsley, Toni Buzzeo, Pat Lowery Collins, Rebekah Goering, Amy Butler Greenfield, David Greenfield, Jennifer Jacobson, A. M. Jenkins, Ginger Knowlton, Jane Kurtz, Jacqueline Briggs Martin, Walter M. Mayes, Mary E. Pearson, Miranda Pettengill, Dian Curtis Regan, Anita Riggio, Maxwell Romotsky, Miriam Rosenblatt, Joanne Stanbridge, F. Peter Waystack, Elaine Werlin, Susan Werlin, Deborah Wiles, Ellen Wittlinger, and Melissa Wyatt.

And thanks, as always, to my editor, Lauri Hornik.

TURN THE PAGE FOR A

rules of survival

DISCUSSION GUIDE

the rules of survival

The *Rules of Survival* is the story of a teenage boy who is trying desperately to save his younger sisters, and himself, from the very real dangers of life with a very disturbing and dangerous woman: their mother. It's a riveting read guaranteed to generate intense discussion among students, not only about the book, but also about real life.

The book's many strengths make the novel a compelling choice for discussion. These include the following:

- Strong, resilient children who protect one another

- Realistic and easy-to-follow language; short chapters make the book more accessible to reluctant readers

- Plot and format draw readers into the story quickly; there is an unusual and involving writing style that uses direct address ("you") as narrator recounts past events to an unseen listener

- Complex, three-dimensional characters that readers can identify with, who have realistically positive and negative qualities

- Adults are shown working together to rescue children from a dangerous and potentially deadly situation

- Provides opportunities for discussion of difficult topics, such as abuse or evil and how to survive it, what constitutes a family, and how children must sometimes be protected from their own families

- The book's risks, which could make the book an edgy choice in some teaching situations, include the facts that the novel portrays a violent and manipulative mother who endangers her children physically and psychologically, a distant and uninvolved father, and some adults who choose to ignore that children are in a dangerous situation.

- There are many ways to survive in a dangerous situation. What are some of the ways Matthew, Callie, and Emmy survive?

- Explain why Emmy prayed for Murdoch. Do you think she realized the effect that it would have on her mother? How might their lives have been different if she had just gone to bed that night?

- Matthew describes Nikki as evil. In what ways do you think she exhibited this quality?

- How did Matt and Callie endanger Emmy by trying to protect her? Speculate on how you think Emmy thought about their mother, both before and after they were separated from her.

- Discuss the scene in which Matthew and Callie saw Murdoch for the first time, what characteristics he showed them in their brief interaction with him, and how that meeting changed their lives.

- Compare Matthew's first view of Murdoch with the way he sees him at the end of the story. What are some of the key events that changed Matthew's perception of Murdoch?

- Why is it that the people you love the most are able to inflict the most pain on you?

- Discuss how the Walsh children's lives were different from and similar to the life of the POW in the movie they watched with Murdoch. In what ways were they prisoners?

- Describe how Matthew and Callie felt when no one would help them. How did those refusals affect them mentally and emotionally?

- Speculate on what might have happened if Ben, Bobbie, and Murdoch had intervened sooner. Would Nikki have been able to stop them and retain control of her children, as Ben feared?

- Nikki knew her children very well, and knew exactly what buttons to push to manipulate them. Give several examples of her ability to do this.

- What were some of the reasons behind Nikki's eccentric and dangerous behavior? What did she gain by acting that way?

- In what ways was Ben a good father? In what ways did he let his children down?

- A number of adults in the book seemed to be afraid of Nikki. What did she do to each of them to make them fear her? What about her frightened them? What about her frightened you?

- There are several turning points in the book where the children's lives get significantly better or worse. Describe them and discuss what caused them and what the results were.

- Why was it so important for the children to pretend the summer with Murdoch had never happened?

What might Nikki have done if they hadn't?

• Why did Nikki takc Emmy away on the day she forced Matthew and Callie to go to church without her? Who was she punishing? Why and how?

• Discuss what Murdoch's quote means: "Some are born great, some achieve greatness, and some have greatness thrust upon them." Give examples of each of these kinds of people. Can you find examples of these kinds of people in the book?

• Why did Aunt Bobbie and Ben suddenly decide to start protecting the children? What caused them to start acting differently?

• Why did Nikki enjoy tormenting Bobbie, both as a child and an adult? What did she gain? How did it affect her children, Bobbie, and Nikki herself?

• On page 126, Matthew describes the scene in which Murdoch commits himself to helping the children. Why did he make that decision at that point? Speculate on what might have happened to him earlier in his life to cause him to come to such a decision at that moment?

• Matthew says he never really learned to trust Aunt Bobbie. Why not? What prevented that bond from forming? What would have had to happen for Matthew to come to trust her completely?

• Every time Matthew realizes nothing has changed in his family, he gets more and more depressed and hopeless. Discuss how future disappointments might have changed the man he would someday become.

• Compare Matt's, Murdoch's, and Bobbie's lives after Nikki got out of jail to living in enemy territory or an active war zone. How would those situations be physically and emotionally similar to what they had to endure?

• Matthew said he changed in the boatyard when he came face-to-face with Nikki. What caused that change, and why did he say that it was irreversible?

• Discuss Matthew's queen bee/mosquito theory. How did the change occur? Are there "queen bees" in your life that you might be able to change to "mosquitoes"?

• How would Matthew's life have changed if he had killed or seriously injured Nikki? How would his sisters' lives have changed?

• Speculate on what will happen to the Walshes, Murdoch, and Aunt Bobbie in the future, in five years, in ten years. What kinds of people will Matthew, Callie, and Emmy grow up to be? How will their childhood experiences affect them as adults? Will Nikki come back? If she does, what effect will that have on her family and their friends?